Harlequin
Presents...

Other titles by

ANNE MATHER
IN HARLEQUIN PRESENTS

Many of these titles, and other titles in the Harlequin Romance series, are available at your local bookseller, or through the Harlequin Reader Service. For a free catalogue listing all available Harlequin Presents titles and Harlequin Romances, send your name and address to:

HARLEQUIN READER SERVICE,
M.P.O. Box 707
Niagara Falls, N.Y. 14302

Canadian address:
Stratford, Ontario, Canada N5A 6W4
or use order coupon at back of books.

ANNE MATHER

dark castle

Harlequin Books

TORONTO • LONDON • NEW YORK • AMSTERDAM • SYDNEY • WINNIPEG

Harlequin Presents edition published April 1976
SBN 373-70635-9

Original hard cover edition published in 1975
by Mills & Boon Limited

Printed in Canada.

CHAPTER ONE

THE train pulled out of the station at Inverness and as its lights disappeared into the misty darkness all Julie was left to look at was her own pale reflection through the window of the compartment. The train was almost empty, but that didn't surprise her. It was not the time of year for holidays, and there was a faint air of melancholy about the empty seats which until a few weeks ago had been full of visitors eager to sample the delights of this single-track journey to the Kyle of Lochalsh.

Not that Julie knew the area or the delights of the journey. Until a few weeks ago she had never even heard of it. But Mark had, and it was Mark's idea that she should come here, and perhaps he had thought the beauty of the scenery might in some way make up for what he was making her do.

She sighed. It had been a long and tedious journey, and she was tense and tired. She had not wanted to come in the first place, and the prolonged hours of isolation in the northbound express had not altered her opinion. She had chosen to travel by train instead of using her car for two reasons – firstly, because she had thought it would be quicker, and secondly, because it would be less tiring. But as the hours had gone by, and the sleeper she had booked for the first stage of her trip had proved of little use to her over-active mind, she had begun to wish she had had the concentration of driving to distract her from the discomfort of her own thoughts.

She shivered. She was cold. She had been waiting at Inverness for almost four hours, and not even the warmth of her sheepskin coat had been sufficient to ward off the onslaught of the chill winds that blew down from the mountains and whistled through the small station. But this train ran only twice daily and although she had only a few more miles to go it was her only link with Achnacraig.

Achnacraig! She stared broodingly out into the darkness. How like Jonas to be so unaccommodating as to put himself almost beyond approach. And yet she would never have imagined him living so far from London, or his beloved Yorkshire, or any of the places he had previously favoured. She knew he still had his apartment in St. James' Mews because she had rung there first, only to be told by the caretaker that Mr. Hunter had left for Scotland some weeks before.

Her hands curled in her lap. She had written, to the address at Achnacraig which his publisher had kindly given her, but Jonas' reply had been brief and to the point. If she wanted to see him, she would have to come to Scotland.

She glanced irritably round the compartment. Her only companions were a red-faced man carrying fishing tackle, and a woman who had probably been shopping in Inverness. Their interest in her had been fleeting and now they both seemed sunk in their own thoughts.

She tried to think positively. She hoped there would be a decent hotel in Achnacraig. She wanted the reassurance of a good meal and a night's sleep before summoning all her courage for the interview with Jonas. She had written and told him she was coming, and if, as she hoped, she could see him tomorrow, she would be able to return to Inverness tomorrow night and complete her journey back to London the following day.

She opened her handbag and took out her compact,

surreptitiously examining her reflection in the small mirror. Wide-spaced hazel eyes, thickly lashed, gazed back at her, slightly shadowed after the restless night spent in the sleeper, while the severity of her hairstyle drew attention to the paleness of her cheeks. She couldn't help wondering whether Jonas would notice any change in her appearance, in the finer contours of her bones, in the hollows of her throat. She was slimmer now than she had been, although not so thin as in the few months after their separation ...

She snapped the compact shut and thrust it back into her handbag. She would not think of that. She was not here to indulge in maudlin sentimentality. This was purely business, and she had no intention of allowing emotion to creep into it. All that had been over long ago, and if Jonas had not uprooted himself and left for some outlandish part of South America before any formal severing of their marriage could be arranged, no doubt they would have been divorced by now.

But she still felt restless. It was all very well telling herself not to think, but the subconscious mind had a habit of disregarding advice. And after all, perhaps it would be better if she did think of what was past, of the way Jonas had behaved, of the humiliation she had suffered at his hands. She drew an unsteady breath. It still hurt – but then pride was a very sensitive thing.

She forced her thoughts into other channels, opening the small briefcase she had on the seat beside her and extracting the file she had begun to compile. She read the bare details she had written with as much detachment as she could summon:

Jonas Hunter is the son of the late Professor Godfrey Hunter, lecturer and statistician. Educated at

7

Winchester and Cambridge, Mr. Hunter joined the staff of a national newspaper after leaving university and achieved considerable success as a journalist. Later he turned to television and became an overseas correspondent based mainly in South America. Recently returned to this country, Mr. Hunter has written a political thriller with all the attributes of a major novel. The novel is to be filmed.

She paused and stared moodily through the window. The train was pulling into a station, but it was not Achnacraig. She watched almost absently as the red-faced man with the fishing tackle left his seat and pushed open the door of the carriage. His departure left only herself and the woman in this part of the train.

There was a whistle and with a jerk the train started away again. With reluctance, Julie forced herself to go on. After all, Mark would expect a good interview from her. Her work was good. She knew that. It always had been. It was the one thing she and Jonas had had in common, although in the end it had been instrumental in driving them apart. But now she must not allow personal issues to stand in the way.

She moistened her lips. After the bald statement of facts she had written – age, description, personal details, etc. She bit her lip. These were things she knew only too well. She hesitated. What she needed to know from him was his motive for writing such a novel, such an indictment of the political system. Had he based his novel on fact, on his own experiences, did it reflect his own views? Then there was the question of whether he was planning another novel, whether indeed he had already started it, and if so, what was it to be about? His reasons behind living in some remote castle in Scotland bore speculation, and finally, what were his plans for the future?

She penned a few brief queries and then closed the file. What a situation, she thought bitterly. Was she mad in coming here? Was any job worth such a sacrifice? Of course, Mark saw no sacrifice in it. So far as he was concerned, her marriage to Jonas had ended when they had separated, and just because he was prepared to use that connection to gain an interview hitherto denied to any other magazine it did not mean that he considered their association in any way binding. And the way he had phrased his request had made it plain that if she wanted to remain his assistant and maintain her position on the magazine she should do this small thing for him.

She put the file back into the briefcase and closed the zip. When she had first written to Jonas about a possible interview she had half expected him to refuse, she knew. That was why she had accepted Mark's ultimatum so calmly. After all, Jonas had refused all kinds of publicity and was fast gaining a reputation for being something of a recluse, a fact Julie had found very hard to believe. All the same, the proof had been there and she had expected her request to be received as unfavourably as the rest. The fact that it had not, that Jonas had actually invited her to visit him in his Scottish retreat for the purpose of gaining an interview, had created a situation which had filled Mark Bernstein with delight and Julie with despair. Jonas's only stipulation had been that she should not bring a photographer with her, that she should come alone. But the worst part of all had been having to tell her mother . . . and Angela.

It was, she supposed, a curious anomaly that she and Angela should have remained friends after everything that had happened. But Angela had wanted it that way, and she had, after all, been the innocent party to Jonas's

9

deceit. When Julie and Jonas split up she had been so upset, so sympathetic, so eager to show how sorry she was that things had turned out the way they did. Julie had still been in a state of shock and in no fit state to withstand the combined persuasions of her mother and Angela, and after a time it hadn't seemed to matter much, one way or the other.

She had a lot to thank Angela for, actually. It was she who had introduced Julie to Mark Bernstein and been instrumental in getting her this job on his magazine, *Peridot*. She had found Julie a flat when she had no longer wanted to stay with her mother, and of course she and Julie's mother were the best of friends. And why not? Angela was the daughter of Mrs. Preston's old school friend, and Julie and Angela had known one another since they were children.

Both Angela and Julie's mother had shared her opinion about her proposed trip to Scotland, and they were more vehement about it.

'I'll speak to Mark,' Angela had said at once. 'He can't possibly expect you to do this. Interviewing a man who was once your husband! It's barbaric!'

'He still is my husband,' Julie had pointed out resignedly.

'And he was unfaithful to you!' Angela had retorted angrily, and not a little cruelly. 'Julie, don't be a fool! This place where he's living is hundreds of miles away. Why can't he come to London if he wants this interview?'

Julie had steeled herself as she had learned to do at the mention of Jonas's infidelity. She was used to hearing Jonas spoken about in this way by her mother and Angela, but it was still possible for certain barbs to pierce the vulnerability of her shell.

Now she said: 'But Jonas doesn't want this interview, Angela, Mark does. You don't suppose Jonas would put himself out for such a paltry reason, do you?'

'But why is he living in Scotland?' her mother had asked. 'I thought his family lived in Yorkshire.'

'They do. And I have no more idea than you why he should have taken himself off to some Scottish fastness, but he has, and that's the situation.'

'If Mark is so eager for the interview why doesn't he go himself?' Angela had persisted, and Julie had found herself colouring.

'Because the interview has been granted to me,' she had had to admit, and had seen the dawning concern in her mother's eyes.

The discussion, if it could be called that, continued, but ultimately they had had to accept that unless Julie wanted to make things difficult for herself she would have to go.

'And why not?' she had challenged bravely, hoping to allay her mother's anxiety. 'Good heavens, we're making far too much of it! Jonas is only a man, Mummy. Just a man – and the accident of our relationship is purely incidental.'

Angela would not let it rest there, however. 'I'll come with you,' she had declared firmly. 'I can get leave of absence from the salon—' Angela was a masseuse, working in partnership with a cousin who was a hairdresser. They had built up a successful salon in the West End, and had many influential names on their books.

But Julie refused to consider her offer. She wasn't feeling at all brave about the coming interview, but she did know that Angela's presence was likely to undermine her confidence, and confidence was something she needed – badly. 'No,' she had averred determinedly, 'you're needed at the salon, and it's about time I was able to stand on my own two feet where Jonas is concerned!'

Angela had protested, of course, and Julie's mother had shed a few tears, but they had both realized that in this Julie was adamant. Perhaps it would do her good to see Jonas again, she had told herself in some of her bleaker moments. Although her love for him had died when she had discovered his duplicity, she had always considered him a fascinating man, and no doubt now that she was older she would see that hero-worship for what it was. She had been only nineteen at the time of their marriage while he had been thirty, and as the marriage had broken up after only a little over two years, she had been just twenty-one then. Now she was twenty-four, and far more capable of assessing a man objectively.

The train was pulling into another station and her nerves tightened, but again it was not Achnacraig. This time her companion got up to leave the train and Julie was alone in the compartment. She sighed, peering through the darkness in an effort to see what was beyond as they left the small station far behind. But the blackness was too complete and she glanced impatiently at her wrist watch. It was a little after seven and she knew that part of her coldness came from hunger. Perhaps she should have stayed overnight in Inverness and travelled on to Achnacraig in the morning. But that would have meant another day, and she was eager to get the interview over and done with and be gone. Even so, it would have given her the added advantage of arriving in daylight, whereas now it could have been midnight if one considered the deserted platforms of the stations they had passed. She hoped that Achnacraig was a little more prepossessing.

Her suitcase was lodged between two seats, so she got up and pulled it out, ready for alighting. It couldn't be much further, surely. She fastened the buttons of her sheepskin coat and looked down at the long suede boots covering her legs to the knee. At least she looked business-like, she decided grimly. She had no intention of allowing Jonas any possibility of imagining that she had come here for any other reason than the given one.

The train was slowing again and Julie pressed her nose against the window pane, drawing back impatiently as her breath misted on the glass. She rubbed it clear and stared at the sign. *Achnacraig*.

Her pulses quickening in spite of herself, she gathered her handbag, briefcase, and the small suitcase she had brought and hurried to the carriage door. But as the train came to a jerky halt it swung open and had she not grabbed the panelling to save herself, she would have been projected forward into the arms of the man standing below her on the platform. He was a tall man, lean and dark-skinned, with overly long dark hair, dressed in a shabby navy duffel coat, dark trousers and wellingtons. Julie stared at him almost disbelievingly, but there was no mistaking the heavy-lidded dark eyes, the high cheek-bones and mockingly twisted mouth with its full lower lip. He had always been a disturbingly attractive man, and she wondered with a fleeting sense of remorse whether women were always more prepared to condemn an attractive man than an unattractive one.

'Jonas!' she managed, as he stooped to pick up the briefcase she had dropped in her efforts to save herself. 'What are you doing here?'

As soon as the words were out she realized how rid-iculous they must sound. He straightened and regarded her humorously.

'Didn't you expect to see me?' he queried sar-donically.

'Well, yes – yes, of course.' She came down the steps on to the platform, looking about her in an effort to conceal the shock he had given her by confronting her so unexpectedly, and he took the suitcase from her unresisting fingers. 'Wh-what I meant was – I – I didn't expect you to meet me.'

'Didn't you?' He glanced down at her. 'But you wrote and told me when you were coming.'

'Yes, I know I did ...' She paused, shivering in the wind that blew through the open ends of the small station. This wasn't at all how she had planned the interview to be. How like Jonas to disconcert her like this, she thought rather uncharitably. 'What I'm trying to say is – I merely wrote so that you would know when to expect me.' She sighed. 'I – I was planning to come and see you tomorrow.'

'Were you?' Jonas didn't sound at all impressed. 'And where were you proposing to spend the night? Or have you got a tent and sleeping bag in your suitcase?'

Julie looked up at him resentfully. 'I intend to spend the night at the nearest hotel or guest-house.'

'Do you?' He had an annoying habit of questioning her every statement. 'Well, shall we go? Old Angus won't welcome you if you keep him waiting to collect your ticket.'

He started away towards the barrier and she had, perforce, to follow him. The wind was tugging wisps of hair from the chignon on the nape of her neck and she tried to tuck the chestnut strands back into place, without much success.

'I – where do you think you're going with my suitcase?' she demanded breathlessly.

Jonas cast an impatient look at her. 'Well, I'm not making off with it,' he returned coolly. Then: 'Ah, here we are, Angus. Last – but not least, as they say.'

As she fumbled for her ticket, Angus cast a dour look in Julie's direction. He seemed awfully old still to be working, but perhaps it was the single swaying light above their heads that cast such shadows across his gnarled face.

'Not much of a night, Mr. Hunter,' he said, and Julie was momentarily distracted by his lilting brogue. 'May be snow before morning, I shouldn't wonder.'

Julie's heart leapt as she handed over the ticket. Snow? In October? Surely not.

She hesitated as the old man was about to turn away, and said tentatively: 'Excuse me . . .'

Jonas stopped some few feet ahead of her and turned, a frown marring his lean features.

'Yes, miss?' Angus looked expectantly at her.

Julie caught her breath. 'I – is there somewhere – that is – do you happen to know where I might find accommodation for the night?'

'Accommodation, was it?' Angus shook his head slowly and Julie's heart sank. Then Jonas was beside her, his hand hard and unyielding about her arm.

'There are no hotels in Achnacraig, Julie,' he said coldly, his eyes daring her to contradict him. 'Besides, I have – accommodation arranged for you.'

Angus had lost interest and was already turning away into his cosy office leaving them alone on the deserted platform. Julie turned to Jonas angrily. 'What do you mean – you have accommodation arranged?'

'Just what I say.' Jonas shifted her suitcase into his other hand.

'At a guest-house, you mean?'

'Julie, there are no guest-houses open in Achnacraig at this time of the year. It's almost November. The tourist season is long over.'

Julie felt upset and frustrated. 'Then where am I to stay?' she demanded, steadying her voice with difficulty.

'At Castle Lochcraig, of course. Where else?'

'Castle – Lochcraig?' Julie gathered the lapels of her coat together with a gloved hand. 'But – but that's your – your—'

'Castle? Yes, I know.' Jonas sounded almost indifferent. 'But don't let that intimidate you. It's not a very large place. Now – my car's parked over here.'

'I'm not coming with you!'

Julie remained where she was, her handbag clutched tightly between her fingers, shivering as much with reaction as cold now. This was the very last thing she had expected. That Jonas should meet her was startling enough. That he should expect her to stay at his castle was – ludicrous!

Jonas shrugged and crossed to where a sleek sports saloon was parked, its expensive outline visible in the shadowy light. He opened the door, tossed her briefcase and suitcase on to the back seat and then levered himself behind the wheel with lithe easy grace. It wasn't until he slammed the door and she heard the roar of the engine that she realized he had accepted her refusal and intended leaving her there. She couldn't believe he would do such a thing, but the sports car was most definitely beginning to move.

'Wait!'

She rushed across the station forecourt and reached his side of the car as he slowed and rolled down his window.

'Yes?'

Julie bit her lip. 'Where do you think you're going?

You've got my suitcase – my briefcase!'

Jonas regarded her from between narrowed lids. He had long thick lashes and they successfully concealed his expression. 'You can collect them tomorrow when you come for that interview,' he remarked dryly.

'Oh, don't be so ridiculous! I shall need my things tonight.' Julie stared impotently round the station yard. 'There has to be habitation here somewhere. Surely someone will put me up for the night.'

Jonas's mouth thinned. 'Don't be so childish, Julie,' he snapped cuttingly. 'What's the matter? Are you afraid to stay at my house?'

'Of course I'm not afraid—'

'Then where's your problem?'

'I'd rather not accept *your* hospitality,' she declared vehemently.

His smile was not pleasant. 'Oh, really? Then I suggest you take the next train out of here. There may be one later. I'm not really sure.'

Julie gasped. 'You can't – you can't mean you'd refuse me the interview after I've travelled all this way . . .' Her voice trailed away into silence.

Jonas tapped his fingers impatiently against the steering wheel. 'Are you going to get into the car, Julie?' he inquired, in ominously level tones.

Julie straightened. She licked her lips and took another look around the dark station yard. The train had departed to continue its journey, and apart from the light in the ticket office, everywhere seemed desolate. She looked down at Jonas again.

'I – that's blackmail,' she protested, shivering uncontrollably.

He thrust open the passenger side door. 'You're going to get pneumonia if you don't make up your mind soon,' he observed. 'Get in. You have no choice, do you?'

Julie's fists clenched. She felt she had never despised anyone as she despised him at that moment. Without another word she walked round the vehicle and climbed into the squab seat beside him, tucking her skirt down over her knees and slamming the door. But she still continued to shiver. Not even the warmth, the reassuring smell of leather and good tobacco, could rid her of that mingled sense of indignation and resentment, and – yes, apprehension.

The car swung out of the yard, its headlights illuminating hawthorn hedges and the narrow road ahead. Once on to the road, Jonas pressed his foot down harder on the accelerator, and the sleek vehicle almost leapt forward. Jonas had always liked travelling at speed, Julie remembered, but he had always been in control and she had never felt nervous with him. Now, however, it was different, and as the road curved first this way and then that, and the headlights caught the winking blackness of a stretch of water on their left, she felt sure he intended plunging them both into its chilling depths.

'Must you drive so fast?' she exclaimed at last, driven beyond bearing by his oppressive silence.

Jonas dropped his speed by five miles an hour and she pressed her hands tightly together. It was scarcely a concession. She turned her head and tried to see some indication of where he was taking her, but there was no sign of life. Just the water, and shadowy clumps of trees and bushes, and occasionally the unexpected glimpse of some night creature. They had covered perhaps four miles already. How much further was Castle Lochcraig?

Presently the car began to slow and a bend in the road brought them to a gravelled area by a stone jetty which jutted out into the murky water. She saw the outline of what appeared to be a boathouse although a few moments later she realized it was a garage – for this car.

Jonas stopped the car, got out and unlocked the garage doors. Julie, the chilliness in her bones dissipated by the tension of the journey, opened her door tentatively.

'Wh-what are you doing?'

Jonas opened the garage doors wide and then said: 'You can get out. This won't take a minute.'

Still Julie hesitated. 'Is – is this it?' she ventured, despising herself for the tremor in her voice.

Jonas cast a disparaging look in her direction, his features clearly visible in the light from the headlamps. 'Hardly,' he commented dryly, and came back to drive the car inside.

Julie hesitated only a moment longer and then got out, watching mutinously as he garaged the vehicle and closed the doors securely. The jetty mocked her and she refused to look towards it. It seemed apparent that Castle Lochcraig was not on the mainland.

'What – what is this stretch of water?' she asked, as he came towards her carrying her cases.

'Loch Craig.'

'A loch? Oh, of course.' Julie sighed. 'I thought it was the sea.'

'It could have been, but it isn't. There are sea lochs, you know, mere continuations of the sea into inland lakes. However, we are some distance from the sea.'

Julie felt suitably reprimanded. It had been a silly statement. The train had travelled inland from Inverness. Jonas walked towards the jetty and in the pale light from a moon tossed about by clouds she saw a small boat with an outboard motor.

'Come on,' he said, unceremoniously tossing her belongings into the bottom of the craft. 'It's not much further now.'

'How reassuring!' Julie spoke with a sarcasm she was far from feeling. 'You didn't warn me that your castle was on an island.'

'Does it matter?' He sounded resigned. 'Look, Julie, you're beginning to annoy me. You asked for this interview, not me. Have the decency to behave like a mature adult. This kind of childish bickering is going to get us nowhere.'

Julie felt her cheeks begin to burn in the darkness, not least because of the truth in what he had said. She had asked for the interview, albeit on Mark's behalf, and since her arrival she had done nothing but argue with him. But that was because everything had gone so horribly wrong, she justified herself defensively. How had she been expected to know that Achnacraig was little more than a halt on the line and that she would be unable to find accommodation? All the same, if Jonas hadn't come to meet her things might have been even worse.

With a reluctant shrug of her shoulders she moved towards the jetty. 'I'm – sorry,' she mumbled ungraciously.

Jonas put out a hand to help her into the boat, making no response to her unwilling apology, and she put her hand into his. Even through the material of her glove she could feel the hard strength of his fingers and for a moment when she dropped down into the boat beside him she was close enough to feel the warmth of his breath against her forehead. A quivering awareness of him spread over her, and as she huddled into the plank seat at the end of the boat she felt resentfully aware that his sexual attraction was as strong as ever. She was glad she had not succumbed to the fleeting desire to wear her most attractive clothes and do her hair in a loose and appealing style. The temptation had been there, to show him that she was not allowing his defection to ruin her appearance, that she was still capable of attracting men, but it had been discarded. And now she was glad it had. She would have hated him to think she was using this interview as a futile means of showing him exactly what he had lost. No, dressed as she was, in her plain city clothes, the thick, waving coil of golden chestnut hair confined in the unbecoming chignon, she would incite no man's interest, least of all a man like Jonas Hunter...

CHAPTER TWO

THE outboard motor started at the first attempt and soon they were moving away from the jetty, bouncing across the wind-choppy water to where a dark mound could just be seen rising out of the loch. As they drew nearer, Julie could distinguish the twin towers of a small castle that stood in the middle of the island, and the thick belt of firs that surrounded it. It stood on a rise, and the ground fell away sharply in places towards a shoreline fringed with jagged rocks like giant's teeth. Julie wondered how on earth anyone could land here, but Jonas circled the island until he came to a shingled stretch, perhaps six feet wide, where he could beach the boat. He stepped out into the water in his boots and dragged the craft up the shingle before offering Julie his hand again to climb out.

The high heels of her boots sank into the small stones as Jonas lifted her cases out of the boat and then drew a torch from his pocket and handed it to her.

'Here,' he said. 'You may need this. I know my way. Just follow me.'

They crossed the stretch of shingle and began to mount steps cut out of the rock. Julie was glad of the light of the torch because the steps were uneven in places and her boots were not meant for climbing. She realized she was out of condition, too, as she began to pant while Jonas strode ahead without any apparent sign of fatigue.

At last the steps gave on to a rough stone walk and looking back she saw that they were high above the rocky shoreline now. Ahead she could see the stone towers she had glimpsed earlier guarding an inner courtyard that was surrounded on three sides by the fortified walls of the castle. A dog barking somewhere at the back of the building was a reassuring sound, as were the lights at some of the narrow windows, but Julie still glanced rather apprehensively at her host.

Jonas stopped at the foot of some steps leading up to an iron-studded door set in one of the turreted towers. Julie followed him slowly as he mounted the steps, gradually regaining her breath after the climb, and entered the panelled hall of the tower. It was almost round, of course, with a passage leading off to the left, and a spiral staircase winding away out of sight. The lighting came from gas lamps which cast a mellow glow over the dark wood. The staircase was stone, as Julie knew the walls to be beneath their panelling, but a soft brown and cream carpet added warmth and colour.

She was still admiring her surroundings when a small dark woman came hurrying along the corridor towards them. 'So you're back then, Mr. Hunter.' The woman's voice was pleasantly accented, with the same brogue as old Angus had used. 'And this would be Mrs. Hunter, of course.'

'Of course.' Jonas had put Julie's cases down and now turned to her with enigmatic coolness. 'Julie, this is Mrs. Macpherson. She and her husband, Rob, have lived and worked here at Castle Lochcraig for over twenty years.'

Julie was still getting over the shock of being introduced as *Mrs.* Hunter. For years she had thought of herself as plain Julie Preston, the name she had always used professionally. That was why she had been so astounded that Mark should have discovered her relationship with Jonas. She had never discussed that period of her life with anyone, not after they had split up, and when Angela had introduced her to Mark it had been as Julie Preston.

But here, apparently, Jonas had explained that she was his estranged wife, and with no small feeling of embarrassment, she shook hands with Mrs. Macpherson and hoped she looked less confused than she felt.

'Your hands are frozen, Mrs. Hunter,' exclaimed the housekeeper, looking reprovingly at Jonas. 'I'm sure you must be tired after your journey. If you'll away with me, I'll show you to your room and you'll have a few minutes to warm yourself and freshen up before I serve dinner.'

Julie forced a smile. 'That would be lovely, Mrs. Macpherson,' she agreed, looking down at her suitcase. 'Shall I bring this?'

'Rob will see to your case, Julie,' said Jonas quietly, divesting himself of his duffel coat, revealing a navy silk shirt beneath. The dark colours accentuated the tan of his skin, heightened no doubt by the years he had spent in South America. The shirt was open at the throat and Julie could see the silver medallion suspended from its slender chain which she had given him for his birthday five years ago. The sight disconcerted her. She would have expected him to have got rid of it long ago. She was almost glad when Mrs. Macpherson touched her arm and said:

'Come along, Mrs. Hunter. It's this way.'

All the same, as they mounted the spiral staircase with the narrow windows let in at intervals, Julie couldn't rid herself of the remembrance of that silver medallion or the memories it so painfully evoked. Memories of Jonas in the first year of their marriage, relaxed and laughing, on that holiday they had spent in Barbados. She had bought him the medallion there and it conjured up memories of Jonas trying to teach her to sail, to go snorkelling and skin-diving – of him asleep beside her early in the morning, when the silver medallion had been his only adornment . . .

Her cheeks flamed and she was glad that Mrs. Macpherson was ahead of her and could not see. She must be mad, allowing such thoughts to invade her head simply because she had happened to see again a cheap piece of jewellery she had purchased in a Bridgetown market. She had to remember that at least one other woman had seen Jonas in that lazily intimate state, and that Jonas himself had been responsible for the destruction of their marriage.

The staircase opened on to a landing with a gallery leading off before continuing on its way, but Mrs. Macpherson indicated that Julie should follow her along the carpeted gallery. The gallery followed the outer wall of the main part of the building and Julie couldn't help noticing how much thicker the stonework was on one side than the other. No doubt in daylight the view from the windows on the outer side would be quite magnificent, but tonight, with the gaslights flickering disconcertingly, it had an eerie atmosphere.

Mrs. Macpherson glanced round. 'All the bedrooms and guest rooms open off the gallery, Mrs. Hunter,' she explained. 'And directly below us is the main hall and dining area, and the reception rooms. Mr. Hunter's private rooms are in the tower where you entered. He doesn't bother much with the formal apartments, although perhaps he will now that you're here.' She smiled encouragingly.

Julie's face felt stiff. What on earth did Mrs. Macpherson mean? Surely it was obvious from the small amount of luggage that she had brought with her that she was not here on a prolonged visit. Hadn't Jonas discussed the length of her stay with his housekeeper? She didn't know how to answer her, so she merely managed a smile and said nothing.

They had passed several heavy doors set into the stonework before Mrs. Macpherson stopped and opened one of them and went inside, beckoning Julie to follow her. The gas lamps here had been turned down, but the housekeeper quickly turned them up and smiled in satisfaction when she saw Julie's obvious admiration of the huge bedroom which they had entered.

From the minute she entered the castle, Julie had realized that some sort of central heating system was in operation, and along the gallery she had noticed huge pipes and an old-fashioned radiator which had definitely taken the chill from the air. But the bedroom was really warm, heated by an enormous log fire burning in an equally enormous grate. There was an immense tester bed, the hanging canopy of which, although faded, bore the unmistakable imprint of years of intricate tapestry work; there were two massive wardrobes and a tallboy full of drawers, a dressing table with five folding mirrors that could throw back one's reflection from every possible angle, and two wingbacked armchairs set at either side of the hearth. The silk-hung walls were unadorned, and overhead the ceiling had been panelled and carved. Julie shook her head helplessly. She had never seen such a bedroom outside of a stately home. But, she supposed wryly, that was exactly what Castle Lochcraig was.

'It's very nice, Mrs. Macpherson. Thank you,' she said.

Mrs. Macpherson waved her thanks away. 'It's good to see the rooms used again,' she protested. 'Mrs. Drummond always slept in this room.'

Julie would have liked to have asked who Mrs. Drummond was, but she thought that perhaps it was something she ought to know, and she decided to ask Jonas rather than question the housekeeper.

'You've a bathroom through here,' went on Mrs. Macpherson, opening an inner door. 'See — it's quite modern.'

Julie peered into the shadowy bathroom. The bath was huge, like everything else here, and the massive, throne-like water closet filled her with amusement. It was good to feel a lightening of her spirits after the day it had been.

'You'll be able to find your way downstairs again, Mrs. Hunter?' The housekeeper paused by the door.

'Oh, yes, I think so.' Julie nodded, glancing at her watch. 'What time have I got?'

'Will twenty minutes be enough for you?'

'I should think it would.' Julie smiled. 'And thank you again. I'm sure I shall be very comfortable here.'

Mrs. Macpherson nodded. 'If you're not, I've no doubt Mr. Hunter will soon let me know,' she commented dryly.

The housekeeper's words aroused just the faintest sense of apprehension, but Julie dismissed the feeling impatiently. Left alone, she was free to explore her domain, but first she would take off her boots and allow her feet to sink into the soft cream carpet underfoot, and warm herself by the fire.

After a wash, she examined her appearance critically. She had shed her sheepskin coat to reveal a plain tweed suit and high-necked white blouse. She had had to put her boots on again as her shoes were in the case downstairs. Her hair needed little attention, the few strands which had escaped from the chignon soon tucked back into place. She applied a light foundation cream to her skin, added a little eye-shadow, and was satisfied with the result. The wind had added a little colour to her cheeks, but it was not unattractive. She sighed. It would be a simple matter to change her image – to loosen her hair and add lustre to her lips, but she restrained the impulse.

With a few minutes to spare she wandered round the room, examining the carvings that were an integral part of the furniture. The drawer handles on the tallboy were shaped like lion's heads and one inserted one's fingers into the open jaws to draw them out . . .

She stood back in surprise. She had opened a drawer, almost without being aware of doing so, and now she stared at its contents. It was filled with filmy lingerie, pants and bras and slips in a variety of shades, fragile chiffon garments and pure silk that clung to her fingers.

She closed the drawer with a jerk and turned away, unaccountably disturbed. Whose garments were they? What were they doing here in this bedroom that Mrs. Macpherson had implied had been long unused? Or had she said that? She had said that the formal apartments downstairs were seldom used, but that didn't mean that no one had used this bedroom. On the contrary, she had said that Mrs. Drummond had always slept here. But somehow Julie knew that the Mrs. Drummond who had always slept here was not the person to wear such extravagant underwear.

Her brows drew together. The articles she had seen were not old. Whose ever they were they had been put there only recently. Had Jonas had some woman staying with him? The idea was distasteful to her. And yet why should it be so? She and Jonas were separated. What he did was his own affair. And if he chose to take some woman as his mistress, it was nothing to do with her.

Even so, there was an awful curling sensation in the pit

of her stomach when she considered him sharing this bed with another woman. If he had, she would rather not sleep in it.

She looked towards the embroidered quilt that covered its enormous width. The bed could have comfortably accommodated half a dozen people, she thought with aversion. Oh, why had she opened that drawer? Like Pandora, she had released something totally unexpected.

She picked up her handbag and walked towards the door, but then she remembered she had not turned down the lamps. She went back to do so and as she passed one of the wardrobes her reflection mocked her. Curiosity was like a cancer inside her and without hesitation she reached out a hand and opened the wardrobe door. Inside were hanging perhaps a score of dresses, both long and short, suits and slack suits, skirts and trousers.

She stared at them in amazement. Surely no woman would go away and leave so many clothes behind her! So what did it mean? That some other woman was still staying at the castle? That she had given up her room to Julie? It didn't make sense.

She turned down the lamps, closed the wardrobe door, and left the bedroom walking swiftly along the shadowy gallery to the spiral staircase. Before going down she looked upward, seeing the spiral disappear towards some upper section of the building. Were there other floors? And if so, did anyone occupy them?

She shook her head. She was becoming fanciful. The sooner she went downstairs and stopped speculating about things that did not concern her, the better it would be.

When she reached the lower hall she looked round. Now she could see that the reason the hall was not completely circular was that two doors had been set into the panelling and beyond them no doubt lay Jonas's private rooms, the rooms Mrs. Macpherson had mentioned.

She was hesitating about which door to open, when a voice behind her said quietly: 'Did you find the accommodation to your liking?'

She swung round to find that Jonas had come along the passage without her being aware of it and was standing supporting himself with one hand against the arched stonework of the aperture. He had clearly washed, too, and combed his hair which now lay smoothly against his head, flicking over the collar of his shirt at the back. He had also added a maroon velvet waistcoat which went well with his dark attire.

Mentally squaring her shoulders, she replied: 'Everything seems very comfortable, thank you.'

Jonas's mouth turned down at the corners and straightening he passed her to open one of the doors she had been hesitating over.

'Won't you go in?' he invited, standing aside for her to do so. 'This is my sitting-room. I spend most of my free time in here. The room next door is my study. We can have a drink before Mrs. Macpherson arrives with our meal. I've told her we'll eat in here this evening.'

Julie entered another strikingly attractive room. It was a curious shape, having three straight walls and one curved one, but its decoration more than made up for its lack of design. A soft apricot and olive green carpet flowed into every corner, no doubt to allay the chill of stone floors, long velvet curtains in matching shades covered the narrow windows, while soft cream leather armchairs and a well-worn cream and green tapestry-covered couch looked superbly comfortable. A small display case contained some exquisite Wedgwood pottery, while the shelves that flanked the fireplace were filled with books and magazines. Another log fire burned cheerfully in the grate and the flames winked on the collection of bottles and decanters which stood on the open flap of a cocktail cabinet. It was an elegant room, and yet it had a relaxing, lived-in sort of atmosphere, and as it was much smaller than the bedroom upstairs it was also less imposing.

Jonas closed the door and nodded towards the chairs and the couch. 'Sit down,' he suggested, walking towards the cocktail cabinet. 'What can I offer you to drink? Sherry? A Martini? Or do you still like Pernod?'

'I'll have a dry Martini, if I may,' she replied, sitting down in one of the soft leather armchairs. Pernod, like the medallion, had too many associations with the past.

Jonas shrugged and turned to pour her drink, pouring himself a generous measure of Scotch as he did so. Then he handed the glass to her and came to sit near her on the tapestry couch, stretching out his long legs towards the fire. He swallowed half his Scotch without any effort, and then looked sideways at her.

'So,' he said, 'and how are you?'

Julie stiffened. 'I'm fine, thank you.'

His eyes assessed her critically, moving over the severely styled hair, the tweed suit, to the slender legs concealed in the suede boots. 'You're thinner. Don't you eat enough – or not often enough?'

Julie endeavoured to return his gaze coolly. She determined not to let him disconcert her again. 'I don't think my eating habits are any concern of yours,' she retorted.

Jonas's eyes were disturbingly intent. 'I thought we had agreed to call a truce,' he commented mildly.

Julie sighed. 'All right. I'm fine. I eat as much as I

need. As far as I know I'm perfectly healthy. Does that answer your question?'

Jonas raised dark eyebrows. 'You're becoming shrewish, Julie. It doesn't suit you.'

Julie looked down at the glass in her hands. She was trembling, in spite of all her good intentions. 'Jonas – I didn't want to come here, to take this interview. It was all Mark's idea—'

'Mark Bernstein?'

'Yes.' She looked up. 'Do you know him?'

'I know – of him.' Jonas felt in his pocket and drew out a case of cheroots. Putting one between his teeth, he said: 'You don't smoke, do you? I'm afraid I can't offer you anything but these.'

Julie shook her head and watched unobtrusively as he reached for a taper and lit his cheroot from the fire. He inhaled with evident enjoyment, and then went on: 'If you didn't want to come here – why did you?'

Julie sipped her Martini. 'You know why.'

'No, I don't.' Jonas shook his head. 'Oh, I admit, I insisted that it was you who interviewed me for the magazine, but you could have refused.'

'Mark would never have forgiven me.'

'And that's important to you?' His eyes narrowed.

'To my career – yes.'

'Ah, I see. Your career.' He swallowed the remainder of his Scotch and rose to pour himself another. 'And is Berstein also responsible for your appearance?'

Julie stared at his broad back indignantly. 'What do you mean?'

He turned, his eyes assessing her again. 'The way you wear your hair – that suit! You used to have excellent dress sense.'

Julie felt herself colouring. 'My appearance is no more

important than my size!'

'I disagree.' He leaned back lazily against the cabinet. 'I think you dressed that way to annoy me. I wonder why.'

'To annoy *you*!' Julie could hear her voice becoming shriller, but there was nothing she could do about it. 'Don't be so ridiculous!'

As it happened, there was a knock at the door then and at Jonas's summons Mrs. Macpherson entered the room wheeling a heated food trolley. She seemed to have noticed nothing amiss, and Julie reflected that the thick walls and heavy doors no doubt cut off all but the most piercing sounds.

'There you are, sir,' she said, spreading a cloth over a side table and drawing it forward. She turned to Julie. 'Shall I serve the meal, Mrs. Hunter, or will you?'

Julie shifted awkwardly in her seat. 'I – er – I can manage, thank you, Mrs. Macpherson. It – it smells delicious.'

'Och, it's only a beef stew with dumplings and vegetables, and there's a syrup pudding to follow,' declaimed the housekeeper with a smile, but it was obvious that she was pleased. 'I'll bring your coffee along later.'

'Thank you, Mrs. Macpherson.' Jonas accompanied her to the door and then closed it behind her.

Meanwhile, Julie was examining the various contents of the heated dishes. The meal smelt even better when she removed a steel lid to reveal a steaming dish of beef stew with tiny dumplings bobbing about its surface.

With a wry smile, Jonas seated himself opposite her, watching her, and forcing a composure she was far from feeling, she said: 'Shall I serve yours?'

'Sure. Why not?' He inclined his head. 'I like most things, you know that. I had to when we first got married, if you remember.'

Julie did remember, but she refused to rise to the bait and ladled some vegetables on to a plate and covered them with the savoury stew. Then she passed the plate across to him and served her own. She gave herself only a very small quantity of everything and was aware that Jonas had noticed. But he didn't comment. Instead, he got up and brought a bottle of wine from the lower compartment of the cocktail cabinet and poured two glasses.

Although Julie had not expected to enjoy the food, she did, and the wine was a pleasing accompaniment. Eating at least curtailed conversation, but she was aware of Jonas's eyes upon her from time to time.

The syrup pudding was as light as any she had tasted, and there was a jug of fresh cream to pour over it. Jonas, she saw, ate with obvious enjoyment, but his lean muscular frame seemed not to be showing any ill effects from Mrs. Macpherson's generous helpings.

Julie finished first and gathered the dirty plates together and put them on the lower shelf of the trolley. Jonas finished his second helping of syrup pudding and lay back, replete, swallowing the dregs of the wine in his glass.

'That's better,' he remarked, wiping his mouth with the back of his hand. 'A few weeks of Mrs. Macpherson's cooking and you'd soon fill out.'

'I have no desire to fill out, thank you,' returned Julie, pushing the trolley aside. 'I was never a filled-out person!'

'No – but you were nicely rounded,' replied Jonas unabashed.

Julie sighed and glanced pointedly at her watch. She was amazed to discover it was half past nine already. 'Er –

34

do you think Mrs. Macpherson will be long with the coffee?' she asked. 'I really am rather tired. I didn't sleep much on the train last night, and I could do with an early night.'

'An early night?' Jonas lit himself another cheroot. 'You disappoint me, Julie. I was looking forward to some after-dinner conversation.'

Julie drew a deep breath. 'I shouldn't have thought you were short of after-dinner conversation, Jonas,' she said sharply.

Jonas frowned. 'No? Why not? Have you no pity for a – lonely man?'

'A lonely man?' Her eyes were drawn to his. 'Oh, come on, Jonas, that's taking things a little too far, don't you think?'

He considered her mockingly. 'Do I denote a trace of maliciousness in your tones?'

'No. No, why should there be?' Julie hunched her shoulders, half regretting her outburst.

'That's what I'm asking myself.'

She sighed. 'Oh, let's stop all this verbal fencing!'

'I couldn't agree more.'

Julie hesitated. 'All right. I – I opened a drawer. In the bedroom. I saw some – clothes.'

'Ah! I begin to comprehend.' Jonas inhaled deeply.

Julie stared at him, waiting for him to explain. But he merely nodded to himself and lay there, lazily blowing smoke rings into the air. She felt angry and frustrated, the more so because she guessed he would know how she was feeling, how eaten up with curiosity she was. But he was not about to satisfy her.

Her hands clenched. Cool down, she told herself furiously. What did it matter? She didn't care whose clothes they were. This time tomorrow she would be long gone, and she hoped she never had to set eyes on him again. She would see her solicitor when she got back to town. A divorce shouldn't be too difficult to arrange, not after all this time, and then she would be free – really free.

Another knock heralded the return of Mrs. Macpherson, this time carrying a tray on which reposed a jug of coffee, cream, sugar, and two cups.

'Now – did you enjoy your dinner?' she inquired anxiously.

Julie forced an enthusiastic note to her voice. 'Very much, Mrs. Macpherson. That syrup sponge was out of this world! You must give me the recipe before I leave.'

'Before you leave, Mrs. Hunter? But you've only just got here—'

'Mrs. Hunter means when we return to London,' put in Jonas smoothly, levering himself off the couch and confronting Julie's indignant stare. 'Thank you, Mrs. Macpherson. We shan't need you any more tonight.'

'No, sir.' Mrs. Macpherson moved slowly towards the door, propelling the trolley before her. 'Oh, by the way, Rob's taken up Mrs. Hunter's cases. I hope you'll be comfortable—'

'I'm sure you've done everything to ensure that,' interposed Jonas patiently, although it was obvious he was eager to have the housekeeper outside the door. 'Good night, Mrs. Macpherson.'

'Good night, sir. Good night, Mrs. Hunter.'

'Good night.' Julie spoke automatically, but as soon as the door was closed she sprang to her feet, and said: 'Exactly what did you mean by that?'

Jonas was calm again, leaning back against the door with indolent grace. 'By what? What did I say?'

'Oh, stop it, Jonas, you know what you said. Look, I don't know what you've told these people – or why you couldn't have introduced me as – as a reporter from *Peridot* and nothing more! But the fact remains that Mrs. Macpherson imagines we're a normal married couple and that I'm here on some sort of holiday!'

'Don't get so heated about it.' Jonas drew lazily on his cheroot. 'You want an explanation? All right, I'll give you one. My grandmother knew I was married. Naturally Rob and Jennie Macpherson knew I was married. Around here, marriage means something.'

Julie shook her head confusedly. 'Your grandmother?'

'Laura Drummond. I inherited Castle Lochcraig from her.'

'*Mrs.* Drummond! Oh! I see.'

'I gather Mrs. Macpherson has mentioned her to you.'

'Well, yes. She – she said that I'm sleeping in her bedroom.'

'That's right. You are. My grandparents always slept in the master bedroom. In the old days, things were done in style. It was my grandfather who had the gallery built on the upper floor. Until then, all the rooms led out of one another, which was rather awkward if one had visitors.' He shrugged. 'My grandfather did quite a lot of modernization one way and another, installing bathrooms and plumbing, central heating . . .'

It explained why the inner wall of the gallery was not as thick as the outer wall, but it didn't really answer her question.

'The Macphersons have never met me,' she protested.

'No. But they did see the wedding photographs. You remember there were photographs. Rather good ones, if I remember correctly.'

'But – but your grandmother wasn't at the wedding.'

'No,' he said again. 'She was very old when she died. Too fragile to travel all the way to London just for the wedding of her grandson.'

'But you never mentioned that she lived in a Scottish castle. That you expected to inherit.' Julie was still groping to find some reasonable motive in all of this.

'Would it have made any difference if I had?' he queried levelly, and her nails dug indignantly into her palms.

'Of course not. You know what I mean.'

'Umm.' He straightened, flexing his back muscles. 'Well, I didn't expect to inherit. The castle has always passed to the eldest heir. My mother, who incidently didn't get on with her mother – my grandmother was a rather autocratic old lady and didn't approve of my father at all – had a brother, my Uncle Stuart. He was expected to inherit. Unfortunately, Stuart never married, and he was killed eighteen months ago in an air disaster in Switzerland.'

'I see.' Julie tried to absorb this. 'Was that when you came back to England?'

'No.' He moved away from the door and as this movement brought him nearer to her, Julie bumped down rather jerkily into her chair again. 'I came back about a year ago. I lived in London for a time, working on my novel, and then when my grandmother died I came here.'

'You – were – in London?' Julie made a helpless little gesture. 'I didn't know.'

'Why should you?' His eyes challenged hers. 'I was the last person you wanted to see, wasn't I?'

Julie looked down at her hands, regretting her momentary lapse. But she had always had the feeling that if ever

Jonas returned to live in London she would know about it, sooner or later.

'I still don't understand why, if it was going to create so many difficulties, you insisted that I came here.'

'Did I say it created difficulties?'

'No, but—' Julie moved her shoulders indifferently. 'So — if I accept your reasons for revealing my identity, unnecessary though they seem, what do you intend telling Mrs. Macpherson when I leave tomorrow?'

Jonas walked to the hearth and stood with his back to the fire, feet apart, the cheroot between his teeth. For a few moments he seemed to be considering what she had said, staring broodingly towards the heavy oak door. Then the dark eyes were turned on her.

'Let's face that when we come to it, shall we?' he suggested evenly.

Julie pressed her lips together. She didn't altogether trust him or his motives. She could imagine her mother's and Angela's horror if they could somehow see her now. In their estimation there would be absolutely no excuse for her being there. And even Julie herself had found no good reason for Jonas's insistence of her taking this interview. Not to mention the disturbing question of those clothes . . .

Her head was beginning to ache from so much confused thinking. With a sigh, she got to her feet again.

'Would you have any objections if I went to bed now?'

Jonas threw the end of his cheroot into the fire. 'But you haven't had your coffee,' he pointed out.

Julie looked down at the exquisitely arranged tray. Mrs. Macpherson had obviously taken a great deal of trouble with it, but she could not stand any more of this ambiguous conversation. She needed to be alone for a while, to absorb what had been said, to try and make some sense of it all.

'I really don't think I want any coffee, thank you,' she replied tautly. 'I know my way to my room. So – so I'll say – good night.'

'Good night, Julie.'

Jonas inclined his head enigmatically and she moved towards the door. For a moment she was tempted to reveal her feelings, to confront him with her fears and suspicions, to see how he would react. But then reason prevailed. Unless she included the summons that had brought her here, he had done nothing to arouse her antagonism. Since her arrival, he had been unfailingly polite, and the accommodation he had provided for her was more than adequate.

Why then did she continually suppose there had to be some ulterior design behind it all? Had her own traitorous reactions to him in some way coloured her reasoning? She had known it would not be easy before she came here. Jonas had been, and would always be, a disturbingly attractive man, and it was natural that she, who had once been his wife in every sense of the word, should still experience a certain amount of awareness of his physical attractions. She could have refused to come, she admitted that now. But she had wanted to prove to herself that anything she had felt for him really was dead, and not just numbed by the shock of his guilt at the time of his betrayal.

She opened the door and looked back at him. He was standing staring into the fire and for a moment was unaware of her scrutiny. There was a curiously vulnerable twist to his lips as he stood there, and something inside her contracted painfully.

With a jerky movement she put herself outside the

door and closed it behind her, closing her eyes for a heart-stopping moment. *No*, she told herself vehemently, no! Jonas knew every trick in the book, and she would not be fooled again.

CHAPTER THREE

WHEN Julie awoke next morning it was to the sound of the wind whistling eerily round the battlemented towers of the castle. The sound momentarily distracted her, arousing a feeling of warmth and security which was quickly dissipated as she remembered where she was. She blinked rapidly and reached for her watch from the bedside table, unable to judge from the dull light probing the heavy curtains exactly what time it might be.

The astonishing discovery that it was after eleven brought her upright in the huge bed, hugging herself as the chilliness of the bedroom swept over her. The fire had gone out and the heating wasn't sufficiently powerful yet to have taken the iciness from the air. She crossed her arms protectively across her breasts, and as she did so she saw a tray of tea standing on the table on the opposite side of the bed.

She frowned, then she leant across and put tentative fingers against the bowl of the teapot. It was cold. Whoever had brought the tea had brought it some time ago. She quivered. Had it been Jonas? Had he stood beside the bed and watched her sleeping? The thought was disruptive, although looking down at the plain cambric nightdress she thought she had been more than adequately covered. But no, it would have been Mrs. Macpherson, and she had clearly decided to let her sleep on.

But now Julie was alarmed. She had yet to see Jonas and conduct that interview with him. She had notes to make and questions to be answered, and very little time to do it in.

She pushed her feet out of bed and stood for a moment looking about her. Then, unable to resist the impulse, she ran across to the window and pushed aside the curtains. The view that confronted her was not inspiring, shrouded as it was by a grey curtain of steadily falling rain, but she could imagine the beauty of the loch deepened to blue by a clear sky, and the distant hills shadowed with purple heather. The mainland was vaguely visible, but it seemed quite a long way away, and there was no sign of life either there or on the fir-clad slopes that fell away below her windows.

With a grimace, she opened the curtains to let a little more light into the room and went into the bathroom to wash. The water was reasonably hot and the activity warmed her. In the bedroom again, she knelt to her opened suitcase and took out some fresh underwear. Then she began to dress, reaching automatically for the white blouse and tweed suit. But they weren't there!

She frowned, shivering a little in her flimsy undergarments, and made a thorough examination of the room. But it was useless. The blouse and suit had disappeared.

Her lips tightened. Someone had taken them away. And she didn't think she had to be a mind-reader to guess who that someone was. She seethed. How dared he? He had criticized her clothes last evening, but that was quite a different matter from stealing them. Or perhaps stealing was too strong a word – confiscating them was nearer the mark.

Her fists clenched. Just what did he hope to gain by it? Did he imagine he had any rights to dictate what she should or should not wear? And what did he expect her to do now that he had taken her only outer garments? She could hardly go downstairs in her pants and slip!

She felt furiously angry, and her weakening response to his assumed vulnerability of the night before seemed like a betrayal of herself. What was she going to do now? She badly wanted to see him, to confront him with his duplicity, but she was confined here because she had no clothes.

She stared angrily round the room, wondering whether she could cover herself with the bedspread, when her eyes alighted on the wardrobe. There were clothes in there in plenty and surely some of them might fit her. Why shouldn't she see if there was something she could wear? Anything was better than having to remain here like a prisoner until he chose to come and release her. Unless . . . Unless he had locked her in!

The thought sent her scurrying to the door, but it opened to her touch and she sighed with relief, closing it again and leaning weakly back against it.

She opened the wardrobe. What should she choose? Something plain and simple, but what? She sighed. It might be as well to see if anything fitted her first. She took out a cream slack suit and pulled on the trousers. They fitted very well, only the waistline being a little big for her. The jacket was the same. It could have been made for her, or perhaps for her as she had once been . . .

She thrust the idea aside and considered her reflection in the mirror. The suit needed no shirt or blouse, and she decided it would do. She suddenly had no desire to try on any more of the clothes.

With trembling fingers she brushed her hair and coiled it on to her nape. But her fingers were shaking so much that she couldn't get the hairpins to stay in place and it kept falling silkily about her shoulders again. She sighed frustratedly. Oh, damn, she thought, was nothing to go right for her today? She would have to leave it loose.

She took another reluctant look at her reflection before leaving the bedroom. The image confronting her was utterly different from yesterday. She had always suited slack suits, and the warm creamy colour accentuated the glow of her skin. The smudges had gone from beneath her eyes and the loosened hairstyle made her look younger than her twenty-four years, deepening the colour of her eyes, drawing attention to the full beauty of her mouth. She was not beautiful, she knew that, indeed it had always been a source of amazement to her that Jonas Hunter should ever have shown any interest in her. Angela was much more his type of woman, tall and lissom, with a classically beautiful face and figure, and the kind of silvery hair that always attracts attention.

But Julie was apt to judge herself rather harshly against Angela's more obvious charms, and failed to realize that the warmth and personality which emanated from her more than made up for a conventionally pretty appearance.

Now she picked up her briefcase and handbag, and balancing the tray with one hand went along the gallery and down the spiral staircase. She could hear the rain beating against the windows as she descended and couldn't help thinking how cosy the castle would be on a winter's evening.

Reaching the hall, she looked about her and then walked determinedly towards Jonas's living-room door. But the living-room was empty and she frowned, setting down the tray, which was beginning to weigh heavily on her arm, on the table where they had eaten the night before. She sighed. Where was he? Then she nodded. Of course – he was probably working. He had told her that his study was next door.

She walked out of the living-room and knocked impatiently at the study door. She was tempted just to barge in, but her confidence would not stretch that far, resentful though she was.

'Good morning, Mrs. Hunter. Are you looking for your husband?'

Mrs. Macpherson's voice behind her was gently querying. Julie turned. 'Oh, good morning, Mrs. Macpherson. Yes. Yes, I'm looking for – for him. Do you know where he is?'

'Of course, madam. He's away to Achnacraig—'

'*Achnacraig!*' Julie was horrified.

'Yes, madam.' Mrs. Macpherson frowned. 'Is anything wrong? He told me you were still sleeping and that he didn't want to disturb you. Was there something you were wanting?'

Julie opened her mouth to tell her, to denounce Jonas and his double-dealing, and then she closed it again. 'I – no. No, not really.' She sighed. 'My – er – the tray's in the living-room. I brought it down. I'm afraid it was cold when I woke up.'

'Ah!' Mrs. Macpherson nodded. 'You slept well?'

'Very well.' Julie was short. She twisted her hands together. 'Er – when – when will Mr. Hunter be back? Did he say?'

'I don't suppose he'll be long, madam,' Mrs. Macpherson smiled. 'If you'll go into the living-room, I'll make you some more tea. Or perhaps you'd prefer coffee. And a lightly boiled egg, perhaps?'

'Oh, really, no.' Julie shook her head. She felt sick. She couldn't eat a thing. 'I – some coffee would be just fine, Mrs. Macpherson, thank you.'

'Coffee it shall be.' Mrs. Macpherson ushered her into the living-room and collected the unused tray of tea. 'Now you sit here by the fire and keep warm. It's a terrible morning. I'll bring the coffee directly.'

'Thank you.'

Julie obeyed. There was little else she could do. She wondered if Mrs. Macpherson had noticed the suit she was wearing and whether she had recognized it as belonging to someone else. She ought to have asked the housekeeper what had happened to her own clothes, but perhaps it was as well not to involve anyone else in what was purely a personal matter.

She seated herself in the armchair where she had been sitting the night before and occupied herself by bringing out the file she had been studying on the train. But somehow the file and its connotations seemed totally unreal this morning.

The coffee was hot, strong, and she drank it black. She needed a clear head and a sharp tongue when Jonas returned. What game was he playing? What the hell did he think he was doing? How dared he take her clothes and then go off to Achnacraig when he must know she would be expecting to speak to him? Speak to him! She felt as if she would like to break his neck!

She looked at her watch. A quarter past twelve. What time did the last train leave for Inverness? She was determined to be on it, clothes or no clothes!

At one o'clock she was pacing irritably about the room when the door opened. She swung round, ready to blaze at Jonas, and found Mrs. Macpherson standing there.

'Och, I'm sorry, Mrs. Hunter,' said the housekeeper apologetically, 'but he's not come back yet.'

Julie made an impotent gesture. 'How much longer do you expect he'll be?'

'I really couldn't say, Mrs. Hunter. When Mr. Hunter gets talking—'

'Talking? Talking to whom?'

47

'To Hamish Alexander, Mrs. Hunter.'

'Hamish Alexander?' Julie frowned. 'Who is he?'

'He's a friend of Mr. Hunter, madam.' Mrs. Macpherson looked concerned. 'Has he not mentioned him to you—'

'I – I—' Julie reddened. 'He may have done.' She sighed. 'And is there any way we can get in touch with them?'

Mrs. Macpherson shook her head. 'Not unless someone goes across to the mainland and contacts them, Mrs. Hunter.'

'And can we do that?'

Mrs. Macpherson cast an expressive look towards the windows against which the rain was driving unceasingly. 'In this weather, madam? The only other boat there is has oars. You wouldn't be expecting Rob to row to the mainland, would you, madam?'

Julie pressed her hands together. 'No ... no, of course not, Mrs. Macpherson. I shouldn't trouble your husband. I'd row myself. I'm perfectly capable—'

'We couldn't let you do that!' The housekeeper was horrified. 'Besides, why should you want to? Mr. Hunter will be back shortly, I'm sure of it. Don't worry, my dear, he'll be all right. I just came to tell you that I've served your lunch in the small dining-room.'

Julie waved a hand helplessly. 'Mrs. Macpherson, I – I—' She broke off. She had been about to tell her that she was leaving that afternoon, but the words stuck in her throat. She turned away, her hands covering her cheeks. Why should she have to make explanations? This was all Jonas's fault. Let him do it.

The housekeeper shifted from one foot to the other. 'Come and have some lunch, madam,' she appealed. 'You'll feel much better with something warm inside you.'

48

Julie squared her shoulders. It was obvious that Mrs. Macpherson saw her concern about Jonas as something utterly different from what it really was. And how could she disabuse her without creating all sorts of difficulties?

She turned back. 'All right, Mrs. Macpherson,' she agreed, resignedly. 'Will you show me the way?'

'Of course.' Mrs Macpherson was clearly relieved. 'And after lunch perhaps you'd like to see over the castle? It's only right that you should know where everything is kept. Since Mrs. Drummond died, Mr. Hunter has left the organization of the household to me, as you know, but now that you're here—'

'Really, Mrs. Macpherson, you carry on!' Julie was fervent. The last thing she wanted was to get involved on *any* level. 'I – we'll discuss it some other time.'

'Very well, madam.'

Mrs. Macpherson seemed genuinely disappointed and Julie reflected that there couldn't be too many housekeepers prepared to give up their authority so thoughtfully. They walked along the carpeted corridor to a small ante-room which had been attractively converted. It was cooler in here, there being no open fireplace, but a gas fire had been placed to throw out as much heat as possible. A circular table had been laid with a spotless white cloth, and a bowl of soup was giving off an aromatic odour.

'I'll go and see about the chicken,' Mrs. Macpherson said, when she had seen Julie comfortably seated. 'Have you everything you need?'

'Yes, thank you.'

Julie managed a smile and picked up her spoon. In a basket beside her, warm rolls smelt delicious, and she found her appetite returning rapidly. It was no use starving herself, she thought, justifying the enjoyment she was getting from the hot soup. She would be far more capable of coping with Jonas with a good meal inside her.

Before she had finished the soup, Mrs. Macpherson returned with a plate of flaky rice on which reposed some golden fried chicken and vegetables, and to finish there was a jam roll.

'I'll get fat,' Julie protested at the end, refusing a second helping of jam roll. 'I'm not used to such enormous meals. Back home, all I have at lunchtime is a sandwich.'

She had spoken unthinkingly and she wished she could withdraw the words when the housekeeper said at once: 'That's because you've been living alone. It's not good for a woman to be living alone. Not when she has a husband to care for. It's unnatural!'

Julie's nerves were taut. 'No – well, my work is in London, Mrs. Macpherson—'

'A woman's place is with her husband,' declared Mrs. Macpherson, and then coloured. 'I'm sorry, Mrs. Hunter. It's nothing to do with me, of course. I'm old-fashioned, that's all.'

Julie rose jerkily to her feet and stared through the window. 'Do you think my – my husband is having lunch with this – this Mr. Alexander?'

'Probably,' agreed the housekeeper, imagining Julie wanted reassurance, but that news didn't reassure her at all. 'It's a shame, and on your first day and all. I expect Mr. Alexander persuaded him to delay his departure to see if the weather would break.'

Julie's fist clenched. She didn't believe *that*. Jonas had left the island deliberately and was delaying his return for the same reasons. What did he hope to achieve? To delay her another day? What good would that do?

She sighed and realized Mrs. Macpherson was still in the room. 'Where will you take your coffee, Mrs. Hunter?' she asked, gathering the dirty plates on to a tray.

Julie shrugged. 'I don't want any more coffee, thank you, Mrs. Macpherson. I – er – I'll help myself to a drink in the living-room, if I want one.'

The housekeeper didn't look altogether approving. Well, if you're sure, Mrs. Hunter . . .'

'I am. The meal was delicious, thank you, and I did enjoy it. But I really don't want anything else.'

'Very well, Mrs. Hunter.' The housekeeper walked towards the door. 'When would you like me to show you over the castle?'

Julie forced a tolerance she was far from feeling. 'Not – not today, I don't think, Mrs. Macpherson.'

The housekeeper said nothing more and Julie felt an unwarranted sense of guilt. But why should she feel guilty? she asked herself impatiently. She had done nothing wrong.

She walked back to the tower hallway, but instead of entering the living-room she looked at the door which Jonas had told her led into his study. His private sanctum was no concern of hers, but he had left her here, and she was entitled to investigate if she chose to do so. Besides, she might even find some clue as to his intentions. On impulse, she turned the handle and opened the door.

The study was of a similar shape and size to the room next door, but it was less comfortably furnished. There were steel filing cabinets and a huge bookcase filled with reference books, while a massive mahogany desk with a leather surface occupied the centre of the plain rusty coloured carpet. A typewriter was standing on the desk, and there were papers and carbons strewn everywhere.

Julie hesitated only a moment and then stepped inside and closed the door behind her.

She walked slowly across the carpet, inhaling the aroma of the small cigars Jonas smoked which lingered in the room. There was no fire in here and the air was distinctly chilly. She stopped by the desk and looked through some papers occupying a wire tray. They were mostly invoices and bills and receipts for accounts settled. A feeling of distaste swept over her, and she had to force herself to walk round the desk and sit down in Jonas's chair. It was made of black leather and swivelled on a single steel pivot. She rode round in it determinedly, then stopped as the feeling of trespass strengthened. No matter how outrageously Jonas was behaving, she had no right to be in here, disturbing his private papers.

Thrusting such discomfiting thoughts aside, she deliberately opened the drawer at the top left-hand side of the desk. Inside were more papers and files of newspaper cuttings, and she closed the drawer again quickly. It was no use. It was not in her nature to pry. Instead, she got to her feet and walked across to the narrow window and peered out.

It was getting dark already, the encroaching gloom of a late autumn day, the sky artificially darkened by the storm. It was still raining and the mainland across the water seemed shrouded in mist. It was impossible to contemplate leaving here alone. She was not used to handling boats, and the possibility that she might get into difficulties and end up in those icy depths filled her with despair.

She turned back angrily, feeding her sense of indignation. Jonas had brought her here and deliberately abandoned her. He might stay away for days and if this weather continued, what could she do about it? Panic rose in her throat, but she pushed it down. What had she to panic about? At least she was dry and warm and well cared for, physically if not mentally.

She tried to think positively. How long would Mark give her before he became suspicious of her absence? One week? Two? She chewed on her lower lip. And what about her mother, and Angela? Would they become concerned if she didn't return in the stipulated few days? She shook her head. Everyone was so far away. And of course, that had been Jonas's intention, too.

She walked back to the desk. She was tempted to take his files and tear them to shreds, anything to release the burning sense of resentment inside her. But her own innate feeling for writing of any kind prevented her from doing something so destructive.

She pulled open the drawer at the opposite side of the desk from the one she had opened earlier. There were papers in here, too, but resting on top of them was a leather-bound diary.

Her fingers ran lightly over the tooled leather, tracing the embossed identification. It was a beautiful piece of workmanship and she wanted to hold it. She lifted it carefully from its resting place and turned it over in her hands. Then she frowned. She had never known Jonas to keep a diary. Notes, yes, but a diary, no. It was too damning a piece of evidence for a newspaper correspondent.

The cover opened and she read the inscription on the front page with a mingled feeling of distaste and self-disgust. It was hard to discern the words in the half light, but she managed it: *To my darling Jonas from your favourite confidante. Use it, I dare you!*

Julie felt a knife-like pain turning in her stomach. So he hadn't changed. Not at all. She was a fool if she had thought he might. He was still getting expensive presents from grateful women. Her lips twisted. And why not? she asked herself bitterly. He had always been attractive to women, he always would be. It was not something he consciously cultivated, it was just there. Wherever he went, women fell over themselves to get near him, to talk to him, to flirt with him, to show him in every possible way that so far as they were concerned he had only to lift one little finger . . .

She thrust the book back into the drawer and slammed it shut. Oh, God, she thought sickly, what was happening to her? How could she probe through his desk like this? What was she becoming? A malicious, bitter woman without either self-control or self-respect.

A knock at the study door made her rigid. 'Y-yes?' she called.

Nothing happened and she realized whoever it was they couldn't hear her. 'Yes?' she called, louder this time and the door opened.

'Oh, you are in here, Mrs. Hunter.' It was Mrs. Macpherson again and Julie was glad of the gloom to hide her embarrassment.

'Yes, Mrs. Macpherson?'

'I – I wondered if you'd like some afternoon tea, madam.'

Julie took a step forward. She sensed the housekeeper's discomfort was as great as hers. 'I think that would be very nice, Mrs. Macpherson,' she agreed. 'I – I'll have it in the living-room if that's all right.'

Mrs Macpherson looked relieved. 'Perfectly, madam. I've lit the lamps in there and I'm sure you'll find it much warmer. It's chilly in here. I'd have had Rob light the fire if I'd thought—'

'That's all right, Mrs. Macpherson.' Julie rubbed her

hands together, realizing how cold she had become. 'I'll come through now.'

The afternoon was drawing to a close and after swallowing two cups of tea and one of the hot, buttered scones Mrs. Macpherson had made, Julie went to stare out of the window again. It was impossible to see anything now. Darkness had fallen, and the wind and rain were still lashing about the castle's sturdy walls. For the first time she felt a twinge of concern for Jonas if he intended returning in this weather. A boat could overturn and be lost and no one would know anything about it until it was too late . . .

She drew an unsteady breath and turned to look at the room. She would not worry about him! He was perfectly capable of taking care of himself. Or what was it they said – the devil takes care of his own? All the same . . .

She couldn't remain in this room doing nothing any longer. She opened the door and went out into the hall. It was much cooler out here and with a sense of despair she mounted the stairs to her room. The gallery was dark and shadowy, and she hurried along it to her bedroom wondering whether she would sleep so soundly tonight if she did not have the comforting thought of Jonas sleeping not too far away. The Macphersons didn't appear to occupy this part of the castle at all and it was rather daunting to consider the thickness of the walls and the lack of penetration any scream she made might make.

But why should she scream? she asked herself impatiently, entering the bedroom. She wasn't afraid of ghosts and no unwelcome intruders could scale these walls.

The fire had been lighted and the lamps, too, turned low as on the night before. She closed the door and looked round miserably. It was hard to remember that less than forty-eight hours ago she had still been in London.

She decided to have a bath to fill in some time and was relieved to find that the water was hot and plentiful. There were bath salts on a glass shelf above the bath and she sprinkled them liberally, sinking into the scented depths with genuine enjoyment.

She must have lain there for the best part of three-quarters of an hour before she summoned the energy to wash herself. Then she emerged and dried herself with the huge fluffy bath sheet, going into her bedroom and standing before the fire, allowing the flames to lick over her soft skin.

Draping the towel sarongwise about her, she put a thoughtful finger to her lips. What was she going to wear this evening? The slack suit she had worn all day – or something more feminine?

She flung open the wardrobe doors and looked impatiently at the garments hanging there. The colours attracted her and with reluctance she pulled out a woollen hostess gown with a high neck tied with a cord and loose flowing lines. It was made of soft lambswool in colours shaded from palest lilac to deep purple and navy. Like the slack suit, it fitted her beautifully, the loose lines concealing her slenderness, hinting at the gentle contours of her figure.

She studied her reflection without pleasure. She still felt resentful at having to wear someone else's clothes, but the gown was so obviously unworn that she did not have the distasteful thought of it covering some other woman's body.

However, seeing the clothes again had renewed her anger against Jonas, and she tugged the brush viciously through her hair, almost enjoying the pain she was inflicting upon herself. She didn't bother to try and arrange her hair in any particular style. She was practically convinced that Jonas did not intend coming back this evening, and no one else was likely to pay her a call.

A sound on the gallery outside her room caused a prickle of alarm to feather along her spine. It had sounded like a footstep and she waited breathlessly for someone to knock at the door. But no knock came, instead the door was propelled inward with deliberate slowness.

She caught her breath and was standing as motionless as a statue when a dark figure appeared in the aperture. A faint cry escaped her as for a moment she thought she was seeing an apparition from the past, a tall lean apparition wearing the velvet jacket, frilled shirt and swinging kilt of his ancestors. Coherency was difficult, but she managed to say in a stifled voice: 'Oh, God, Jonas – you – you terrified me!'

CHAPTER FOUR

JONAS stepped indolently into the room and closed the door, looking about him with casual interest before concentrating his attention on Julie. In the formal Highland dress he looked every inch a Scottish baron and she found her senses responding unwillingly to his disturbing masculinity.

But then anger came to her rescue, and she exclaimed: 'Just what game do you think you're playing, Jonas?'

He looked at her, his eyes dropping insolently down the length of her body. 'Am I playing a game?' he asked mockingly.

'That's what I want to know.' Julie put a hand to her throat. 'Jonas – Jonas, you had no right to leave me here alone all day!'

His eyes were darkly amused. 'I'm sorry.' He walked across to the hearth, his kilt swinging about his strong legs. He turned to face her. 'I didn't realize you desired my company so urgently.'

'Jonas, stop this!' Julie took a deep breath. 'You know what I mean. You're deliberately misunderstanding me.'

'I'm delighted that you look more like my wife this evening,' he commented, ignoring her protests. 'Don't you think I have very good taste?'

'You – chose – this?' She stared at him in dismay.

'Yes.' Jonas tucked his thumbs into the pocket of his black velvet jacket. 'Don't you like it? You should. It suits you.'

Julie looked at him through a mist of anger and disgust. 'You're despicable, do you know that?' she stormed violently. 'How can you stand there and tell me—'

'Cool it, Julie!'

'No, I will not cool it! Boasting to me about buying clothes for your – your *mistress*! You're disgusting! How many have there been now, Jonas? Anyone else I know?'

Jonas's mouth turned down at the corners. 'Why do you ask that?'

Julie's brows quirked. 'You know why. Don't tell me you're still going to deny it.'

His lip curled. 'I wouldn't attempt to do so.'

'That's just as well, because you'd be wasting your time. And what about your favourite confidante?'

Jonas's jaw was taut. 'What do you mean?'

'Surely you know. Surely you recognize the phrase.' Julie plucked at the folds of her gown. 'It's as good a description as any, I suppose. Who is she, Jonas – *darling Jonas*?'

'Have you been in my study?'

If she had not been so incensed, Julie might have detected the sudden grimness of his tones. 'What if I have?' she taunted. 'What are you going to do about it? Why shouldn't I poke around? You do it all the time, don't you – *darling*?'

Jonas's features were set. 'You have no right to go into my study—'

'No right?' Julie gave a scornful laugh. 'Oh, really, you're a great one to talk about rights, aren't you? Bringing me here – taking my clothes – forcing me to stay when you knew I wanted to go!'

'I needed to talk to you,' he muttered, in a curiously strained tone.

'Did you?' Julie grimaced. 'Well, you have a peculiar

way of behaving for some one who wants to talk. Disappearing all day – deliberately staying out of sight until it was too late for me to get back to Inverness—'

'You don't understand.'

'No, I don't—'

'The outboard motor failed—'

'Oh, honestly, Jonas, can't you do better than that?' Julie was past being reasonable. 'I'd have invited a cloudburst, at least!'

'It's the truth!' His voice should have warned her that he was nearing the end of his tether.

'What do you know of the truth? You're so used to telling lies, I doubt whether you'd know the truth if you heard it!'

'Julie, I warn you—'

'You – warn – me?' she gasped. '*I* warn *you*, Jonas, I'm leaving in the morning, interview or no interview. I shall tell Mark that your only motives for bringing me here were to hurt and humiliate me!'

'For God's sake, Julie, listen to me—'

'I don't want to listen to you.' She caught her breath on a sob. She mustn't break down now. Not when she was winning. 'I just want you to get out of here. You can tell Mrs. Macpherson I don't want any dinner—'

Jonas's hands withdrew from his pockets, balled into fists. 'That is enough, Julie,' he said, his eyes glittering strangely. 'You have made it clear that whatever I say – whatever justification I offer – will be met with the same response.'

'What did you expect?' Julie's mouth worked tremulously. 'Oh, go away, Jonas, I don't want to talk to you any more.'

She turned her back on him, her breathing ragged. She could feel the pricking of tears behind her eyes and she thought that after he had gone she would not be able to resist giving in to them. It was foolish and stupid and totally unnecessary, but she couldn't help it. Jonas had always had this devastating effect on her emotions.

She waited for him to leave with growing unease. She couldn't remain composed for much longer, and it would be complete ignominy to break down there in front of him. How he would enjoy that, how it would amuse him to relate this scene to someone else, some other woman . . .

She heard him cross the floor and a little of the tension went out of her. But he didn't get to the door, and a few moments later she felt his breath fanning the back of her neck. She could smell the faint aroma of whisky, too, that warned her he had been drinking.

She stiffened, a terrifying feeling of helplessness sweeping over her. But no, she told herself weakly, Jonas wasn't like that, he wouldn't do anything to hurt her. But he had, a small voice inside her insisted. He had been unfaithful to her with her best friend! What greater humiliation could there be? How could she expect any mercy at his hands?

When his hands descended on her shoulders, she struggled like a wild thing, getting away from him and putting the width of the bed between them. He had shed his velvet jacket and the frilled white shirt threw his tanned face into more prominence, darkening his skin and hardening his eyes. His eyes frightened her. They were completely cold, ruthless and utterly determined. He stood facing her, leant slightly forward, his hands resting on the quilt at his side of the bed.

'I – I – I'll – sc-scream!' she stammered.

'Go ahead. The walls are thick. They can stand it.'

'Wh-what do you think – you – you're doing?'

'Grow up, Julie!'

'You won't get away with it.'

'Won't I? Who's going to stop me? Not Mummy – or dear friend Angela!'

'I – I'll never forgive you—'

'You won't anyway.' His lips twisted. 'You've already told me you're leaving in the morning.'

Julie licked her dry lips. 'I – I won't. I'll stay—'

'Don't make a fool of yourself, Julie. You can't escape me. It's stupid to try.'

Julie measured the distance between where she stood and the door. He was nearer. What possible chance did she have of reaching the door, opening it, and getting away before he caught her. And this long dress – it could only be a hindrance. Again she blamed him for taking away her clothes. In her suit she might have had half a chance.

'Don't do it, Julie.'

It was almost as though he could read her panic-stricken thoughts and she could feel her heart hammering sickeningly against her ribs. She saw him lift his foot to the bed and realized he intended to vault across it to reach her. She turned and ran wildly for the door, a little bubbling gasp rising in her throat. The long dress was more than a hindrance – it tripped her, and she sprawled at his feet, helplessly groping for the door as he came round the bed and stood over her.

She lay there, sobbing as much with frustration as fear, but when he came down beside her, imprisoning her hands with one of his and encircling her throat with the other, real terror gripped her. His hand gathered up the cord of her gown and pulled it tightly until it was cutting into the soft skin of her neck.

'Jonas—' she choked, turning her head from side to side, and his eyes darkened contemptuously.

'I could kill you, do you know that?' he muttered savagely. 'What do you think I am – an animal? Have you been so completely brainwashed that you imagine I would *rape* my own wife? Oh, yes, I see you have. Your mother and Angela have done their work well, haven't they? You really believe the worst of me, don't you, Julie? Do you hate me? Do you despise me? Just what did they tell you?'

'Jonas, please . . .' The words were despairing.

He stared down at her angrily, his eyes moving over her without compassion. But then his fingers extracted themselves from the narrow cord and she could breathe freely again. He turned away from her, his shoulders hunched, his knees drawn up, his arms wrapped round them.

Julie scrambled to her feet while she could. Lying there, looking at his evident dejection, she had felt an almost overwhelming temptation to touch him, and such feelings must be controlled at all costs. She went across to the mirror and surreptitiously examined her neck. The mark of the cord could be clearly seen and she drew the neckline of the gown higher to hide it.

Jonas got to his feet and walked across to where he had slung his velvet jacket on an armchair by the fire. He picked it up and put it on, smoothing a hand over the thick vitality of his hair. Then he looked at Julie.

'We will dine downstairs,' he stated grimly. 'Is that understood?'

Julie swung round. 'My neck . . . Mrs. Macpherson is bound to notice . . .'

Jonas shook his head. 'I doubt it. But if she does, you can tell her that you must have tied the cord too tightly.'

Julie pressed her lips together. 'And if I refuse?'

Jonas walked broodingly towards the door. 'I don't somehow think you dare,' he replied coldly, and left her.

After he had gone, tears would not come. She was just as fraught with tension as before, but now it was different. Now she couldn't give in to self-pitying tears. Her eyes felt dry, and the lump in her throat was a painfully physical thing.

When she finally summoned up the courage to go downstairs it was to find Mrs. Macpherson already serving dinner from the trolley on to the small table in the living-room.

'Och, so there you are, Mrs. Hunter,' she chided, with a rather knowing look. 'It was getting late, so I thought I'd save you the trouble of doing this.' She smiled. 'And you see, here he is, back safe and sound. All that worry was for nothing, wasn't it?'

'Worry, Mrs. Macpherson?'

Julie was looking at her watch, staggered to find it was already after nine o'clock, but she heard the question in Jonas's tones as he challenged the housekeeper's statement. He was standing before the fire, feet apart, and Julie's eyes were unwillingly drawn to the powerful muscles that rippled beneath the swaying elegance of his kilt.

'Why, of course, sir.' Mrs. Macpherson straightened from setting out some delectable-looking savoury pancakes. 'I think Mrs. Hunter was feeling rather neglected.'

Julie coloured and Jonas gave the housekeeper a faint smile. 'You could be right, Mrs. Macpherson. Oh, and by the way, will you tell Rob that the starter motor's sticking again. I had the hell of a job to get it to work at all.'

'Oh, yes, sir.'

Mrs Macpherson nodded, and Julie turned deliberately to a magazine lying on the chair where she had left it earlier. She had no doubt that Jonas's statement had been for her benefit, and she wondered whether Mrs. Macpherson was a party to the deception or whether the outboard motor had really failed.

'Will that be all, Mr. Hunter?'

Mrs. Macpherson was leaving and Jonas saw her to the door. When it was closed behind her, he came back to the table and said: 'Will you come and sit down? Or are you going to pretend to read that magazine all evening?'

Julie put the magazine away and came to her chair, sitting down abruptly and looking down at the savoury pancakes on her plate. Jonas seated himself opposite her and picked up his knife and fork. He tackled the pancakes with determination and with a sigh she picked up her cutlery and tried to do the same.

But tonight her appetite really was lacking, and not even the dry wine he poured for her could stimulate her palate. There was a roast of beef to follow, with Yorkshire pudding and vegetables, and Mrs. Macpherson had made the puddings in cake tins so that they were small and crisp. Julie made a concerted effort to behave normally, but only the lemon soufflé which completed the meal would slide down unaided. She noticed that Jonas did not eat as enthusiastically as he had done the night before and she felt suddenly guilty.

After all, everything that had happened since she came here had been put out of context by her overcharged imagination. Even today, when she had been hating him for staying away, the motor on his boat had apparently failed. Something entirely beyond his control.

She bit her lip. Where had she gone wrong? Just because he had met her at the station and told her she would have to stay at his house she had allowed the whole affair to escalate into a ridiculous farce that seemed to have no roots except in her own brain. This morning she *had* overslept, and he could have been back from Achnacraig before she was even aware that he had gone. Only the clothes in the wardrobe and the lingerie in the tallboy drawer struck a discordant note. Who did they belong to?

She looked up, pushing her dessert plate aside. Jonas had already left the table and was bending to light a cheroot with a taper from the fire. Her eyes encountered his as he turned and she faltered at the coldness in their depths.

'Jonas,' she began uncomfortably, 'Jonas, I want to apologize . . .'

'Do you?' He inhaled deeply. 'I shouldn't bother. Apologies are never fully meant or fully accepted.'

'Mine are!' She sighed. 'Did the outboard motor really fail?'

He walked across to pour himself some brandy. 'Will you have a liqueur?' he asked politely.

'No.' She was impatient. 'Jonas, I asked you a question.'

He brought the brandy goblet back to the couch and seated himself, cradling the spirit between his fingers. 'I told you what happened,' he said expressionlessly.

'I know what you said . . .' Julie rose now and walked restlessly across the hearth. 'Jonas, whose are those clothes upstairs?'

He looked down into his glass. 'Whose do you think they are?'

'I've no idea. That's why I'm asking you.'

'All right. Whose do you suppose they are?'

'Well, they're some woman's, obviously.' She looked down at the toes of her shoes. 'I – I can't be expected to know who you've had staying here with – with you, can I?'

'It never even occurs to you to wonder whether there might not be some purely innocent reason for their being there, does it?' he demanded bitterly, pinning her with his eyes.

Julie shifted uneasily. 'What – what innocent reason could there be?' she challenged.

'They could be – my sister's.'

'You don't have a sister.'

'All right. A cousin's, then.'

'What cousin?'

'Does it matter? I'm merely quoting you hypothetical answers to your question.'

'So they don't belong to your cousin?'

'I never said they did.'

Julie bent her head. 'The fact remains, they're there, and you won't tell me whose they are.' She looked up. 'How can you expect me to trust you when you behave so – so deceitfully?'

Jonas swallowed his brandy at a gulp. 'Trust is a word you don't know the meaning of,' he stated bleakly. 'So far as you are concerned, trust has to be seen to be believed!'

'Stop exaggerating—'

'Oh, I'm not. I've known of wives trusting their husbands when it's been blatantly obvious that the husband is guilty of whatever he's been accused.'

Julie had to defend herself. 'Isn't that rather naïve—'

'Perhaps. But if you love someone, you're usually prepared to give them at least the benefit of the doubt.' He tossed his glass carelessly. 'Oh, but I was forgetting something – there was no doubt in your mind, was there? You had Angela's word, and that was much more trustworthy than mine, wasn't it?'

'Jonas, Angela was terribly upset—'

'God in heaven!' He sprang to his feet. 'Do you think I was not?'

'It's different for a man—'

'What the hell do you mean, different for a man? When nothing happens, what difference is there?'

'Oh, Jonas, please, don't start that all over again—'

'Why not? Am I not entitled to a hearing? Is that it?

'No, of course not.' Julie spread her hands. 'But I know the facts, Jonas. There's no refuting them. Besides, I've known Angela since I was a very small girl. We're very fond of each other. I – I *know* her.'

'You knew me, too.'

She turned away. 'I thought I did.'

'You did! Julie, have you forgotten what we meant to each other?'

'Oh, Jonas, we were married. But we'd only known one another for two and a half years!'

'Might I point out that we're still married?' Jonas's face was taut and angry. 'We've now known one another for five years. What difference does time make, you tell me.'

'That's different. We've been apart—'

'Unfortunately, that's so.' He nodded. 'Through no fault of mine.'

'How can you say that?' She stared at him incredulously. Then she shook her head. 'Please, Jonas, I don't want to fight with you again. I didn't come here to start a debate about something that was all over long ago. In — in fact, when I get back to London, I intend to see a

68

solicitor.'

Jonas's fingers were gripping his glass so tightly that it suddenly cracked and splintered, shattering in his hand. The stem fell to the floor and Julie watched in horror as blood began to pour on to the carpet.

'Oh, Jonas!' She rushed forward, grasping his wrist and turning his hand palm upward. 'Jonas, look what you've done!'

'Leave it!'

He was drawing away from her as the door opened and Mrs. Macpherson came in with their coffee. She saw the blood dripping from Jonas's fingers and gasped in dismay. Thrusting down the tray on the nearest resting place, she came across to them, brushing Julie aside and gripping his wrist tightly, momentarily slowing the flow of blood to his hand.

'Do you have a large handkerchief?' she asked efficiently, and Jonas reluctantly pulled one from his pocket.

Julie watched as the housekeeper applied a tourniquet, wondering why she hadn't done something useful like that instead of just exclaiming over his injuries. His hand was a mess of blood and glass splinters and she badly wanted to do something to help him.

But Jonas didn't even look at her, and Mrs. Macpherson finished tying the handkerchief in place and said: 'Come away with me, Mr. Hunter. Rob will attend to this.'

Jonas protested that he could manage, but it was a very desultory protest, and they both left the room leaving Julie alone. She walked restlessly across the floor wondering whether the Macphersons would think it strange that she should not have gone with Jonas. But how could she force her presence upon them when Jonas had so clearly wanted no help from her?

It seemed hours before she heard anyone returning and she spent part of the time cleaning the blood from the carpet. She couldn't make a very good job of it without any cleaning materials, but at least the stain would not show so obviously. She threw the handkerchief of her own she used on to the fire afterwards, and watched as the flames licked round the scarlet stains. Her lips trembled. It was like destroying part of him.

She could have gone to bed, but she didn't. She had to know whether his hand was going to be all right. It was his right hand, his writing hand, and she wished she didn't feel so responsible.

At last she heard someone coming along the corridor. She had left the door ajar so that she could hear the slightest sound, and now she went towards it, halting uncertainly when Jonas came into the room. His hand had been extensively bandaged, from his fingers to his wrist, and his pallor bore witness to the amount of blood he had lost. He ignored her and walked straight to the drinks cabinet, pouring himself a stiff Scotch with his left hand, and swallowing it before turning. Then he poured another and carried it with him to stand before the fire.

'Why are you still here?' he asked harshly, looking at Julie. 'I expected you would have gone to bed by now.'

Julie twisted her hands together. 'I – I couldn't go, not – not knowing whether your hand was going to be all right—'

'My hand is fine, thank you. Rob Macpherson is an excellent first aid man. I'll survive – much to your regret, I'm sure.'

'Oh, Jonas!' Her lips moved protestingly. 'Jonas, you know that's not so.'

'Do I? What difference would it make to you? We

haven't seen one another for over two years. I could have been dead for all you cared.'

Julie felt sick. 'Jonas, that's ridiculous, and you know it. I – I knew you weren't – dead. You sent reports . . .'

'Oh, yes. And you watched them, I suppose.'

'Some of them.' Julie nodded. How could she tell him that in the beginning she had been unable to look at him without feeling ill? 'Anyway, I'm glad that you're going to be all right. I think you ought to see a doctor, though. Splinters of glass can be dangerous.'

Jonas considered her anxious face for a few moments, and then he said: 'And how am I to get to the doctor's? My doctor is in Newton Carn, fifteen miles away.'

Julie frowned. 'Mr. Macpherson will take you.'

'Rob? Have you seen him? No, I thought not. Rob has only one leg, Julie. He doesn't drive.'

'Mrs. Macpherson, then.'

'What possible reason would Mrs. Macpherson have for learning to drive? They don't own a car.'

Julie sighed. 'I'll take you.'

Jonas's eyes narrowed. 'Will you? I thought you were leaving in the morning.'

Julie made a helpless gesture. 'Yes. Well, I can't can I?'

'Why not? It wasn't your fault.'

She stared frustratedly at him. 'Do you want me to go?'

Jonas held her gaze. 'No. I want you to stay.'

Julie's heart thundered against her ribs. She was letting him disconcert her again. She must not do that. If she was to stay another couple of days and take him to Newton Carn she must be sure she could remain in control of herself. She must remember he was an expert when it came to getting what he wanted . . .

She held up her head. 'All right, I'll take you to Newton Carn. And if you're still prepared for me to interview you, I'd like to do that tomorrow afternoon. I'll leave on Friday.'

Jonas raised his glass to his lips in a somewhat mocking salute. 'You're very kind.'

Julie coloured. 'I'm not kind at all. I – I'm just sorry that it happened.'

'Thank you.'

'Don't thank me!' She turned abruptly aside. 'I think I'll go to bed now.'

'We never seem to drink Mrs. Macpherson's excellent coffee, do we?'

'Oh!' Julie paused. 'Do you want some? Shall I pour it for you?'

'Yes. Yes, why not?' His lips curved sardonically. 'Black with sugar. Plenty of sugar. Isn't that supposed to be good for shock?'

'You must be over the shock by now,' she exclaimed, busying herself setting out the cups.

'That rather depends which shock you're referring to,' he commented dryly.

She looked up curiously. 'What do you mean?'

He shrugged his broad shoulders. 'You agreeing to stay?'

She pressed her lips together. 'Oh, that's stilly.'

'Why is it? Mummy and Angela won't approve!'

Julie straightened impatiently. 'Jonas, do you want me to go?'

'I've told you what I want.'

She looked down again, aware of the unsteadying influence of his nearness. He was doing this deliberately, playing on her emotions, and she must not let him get away with it. She poured the coffee, added two heaped spoons of brown sugar, and held out the cup.

'There you are, then. Can I go now?'

He took the cup. 'Won't you join me?'

'No, thank you.'

He inclined his head. 'Sleep well.'

She walked to the door and then paused, a thought occurring to her. 'Jonas – where are my clothes? I – I'd like to wear them.'

'While you're here?' He shook his head. 'I'll see that they're returned to you before you leave.'

'That's not good enough!'

'I'm afraid it will have to be.' The steel was back in his eyes again.

Julie hesitated only a moment longer and then realizing that in any battle of wills he was likely to get the better of her she went out, closing the door with an angry click. It was only as she was mounting the spiral staircase that she realized it must have been he who had entered her bedroom with the tray of tea that morning and taken away her clothes while she was sleeping. The knowledge was disturbing.

CHAPTER FIVE

THE following morning Julie was up just after eight and was in the bathroom when she heard someone moving about in the bedroom. Wrapping a bath towel closely about her, she went to the door and peeped nervously into the room. Mrs. Macpherson was just straightening after placing a tray of morning tea on the bedside table, and Julie sighed with relief before going into the room.

'Good morning, Mrs. Macpherson, thank you.'

'Oh, good morning, Mrs. Hunter.' The housekeeper turned to look at her. 'Is Mr. Hunter up and about already?'

'Up and – about—' Julie hoped she hadn't sounded as astounded as she felt, but realization of what the house-keeper meant was slow in coming to her.

'I'm here, Mrs. Macpherson.' Jonas's voice from the open doorway startled her even more. He entered the room stretching lazily, the bandage on his hand very white against the dark blue wool of his dressing gown. 'I was – er – just using the bathroom next door.'

Julie turned away in embarrassment, wishing she had stopped to put on some clothes before coming so impulsively into the bedroom to speak to Mrs. Macpherson. But she had not dreamed that Jonas might be expected to appear. She couldn't decide whether she was glad or sorry that he had. Without his intervention, she might have found it very difficult to find some reasonable explanation for his absence to give to Mrs. Macpherson, but perhaps it would have been better for the housekeeper to have become suspicious that everything between them

74

was not as it should be. As it was, in the fine wool dressing gown, his bare legs and feet revealing that it was all he wore, his dark hair tousled and the shadow of stubble on his jawline, Jonas seemed very much at home in this room, and she found she resented it.

'I see,' Mrs. Macpherson was saying now, her tone indicating what she thought of married couples using separate bathrooms. 'And did the pain in your hand keep you awake last night?'

'Nothing keeps me awake, Mrs Macpherson.' Jonas smiled crookedly. 'We'll have breakfast in half an hour, if we may. Oh, and by the way, Mrs. Hunter is going to drive me to Newton Carn this morning to see old Mc-Tavish.'

'I think you do right to see the doctor, sir.' Mrs. Macpherson nodded. 'You can't be too careful with glass.'

'No.' Jonas accepted this. 'It's not still raining, is it?'

'No, sir, it's a fine morning. Cold, but brisk.' Mrs. Macpherson flicked an encompassing look at both of them. 'Well, I'll leave you now to have your tea. And Rob will have the boat ready before you leave.'

'Thank you, Mrs. Macpherson.'

Jonas followed her to the door and closed it behind her. Julie, suddenly realizing how cold she felt, marched determinedly to the bathroom. Then she stopped. She had no clothes in there, only her nightdress!

'Will you leave now?' she requested shortly.

Jonas yawned and walked towards the bed. 'I don't think I'd better. Not just yet.'

'But how did you know she was here?' Julie protested.

'My room is next door,' he replied, sitting down on the side of the bed and reaching for the teapot with his left hand. '*Damn!*' He burned his fingers and set it down

75

again heavily. 'I heard her coming along the gallery.'

Julie hesitated, watching his fumbling ineptitude, and then walked across to the tray, assuring herself that the towelling sarong was firmly secured. 'Would you like me to do it?'

He looked up at her. 'Yes, please.'

Refusing to meet the amused mockery in his eyes, she set out the cups and picked up the teapot. Obviously Mrs. Macpherson had prepared the tea for both of them – two cups and saucers, cream and sugar, at least a dozen home-made shortbread biscuits.

While she poured the tea, Jonas ate one of the biscuits. 'Try one,' he suggested as she straightened. 'They're very good.'

Julie looked down at him. 'You're going to get fat.'

'Am I?' He unloosened the cord of his dressing gown and before she could turn away he exhibited his lean torso. 'Do I look fat?'

Julie walked rather jerkily across to the bathroom. 'I'm going to finish washing. I – I expect you to be gone when I come back.'

'You haven't asked me how my hand is this morning,' he remarked, fastening his dressing gown again.

Julie sighed. 'So how is it?'

'It feels painful when I move my fingers. The skin feels tight. It's an unpleasant sensation.'

Julie looked helplessly at him. 'Then it's just as well you're going to see the doctor, isn't it?'

'Umm.' He swallowed a mouthful of his tea. 'Ugh, did you put any sugar in this?'

'You're not completely helpless,' she exclaimed impatiently. 'The sugar's there – use some!'

Jonas shrugged and complied, spooning several generous measures into his cup. 'That's better.' He smiled across at her, and when he wasn't mocking or angry, his smile was quite devastating. 'Did you sleep well?'

Julie could feel heat sweeping over her body from the tips of her toes to the top of her head. 'Jonas, get out of here,' she pleaded.

'Why?' He put his teacup back on to the tray and stretched his length on her bed, looking appraisingly at her. 'I've enjoyed my tea, and you're adequately covered. You always did look good in the mornings, without make-up and your hair all tangled like that.'

Julie's legs were trembling so much she didn't know how they continued to support her. Without looking at him again, she walked to the wardrobe and opened it. Once she was dressed she would feel less vulnerable.

As she looked at the atttractive garments she wondered in amazement how this situation had been allowed to come about. In London it had seemed like an unpleasant, but straightforward, assignment. But she had not allowed for the personalities involved. If either her mother or Angela should learn that she had spent three nights at Jonas's castle, and it would be three nights if she stayed until tomorrow as she had promised, they would think she had taken leave of her senses. There was nothing stopping her from walking out of here right now, so why didn't she?

She extracted a pair of dark green corded pants and a lemon yellow roll-necked sweater and turned round determinedly, prepared to order him out of her bedroom if necessary. Jonas was still lying on the bed, but his eyes were closed, and there was something defenceless about bare feet and the way his gown had parted to reveal the hair-roughened skin of his chest. Her senses responded violently to his undoubted sensuality and with clenched jaws she marched into the bathroom, slamming the door after

77

her, uncaring that she had probably disturbed him after all.

When she emerged he had gone and she felt furiously aware that she was disappointed. Oh, God! she thought bitterly. He certainly knew how to play this game. Much, much better than she did!

Over breakfast which they took in the dining-room where she had eaten the day before she deliberately talked about her work in London, describing the interesting aspects of having a weekly deadline instead of a daily one. She told him about parties she had been to, people she had met, some of whom were well known to him, men she had been out with. The fact that there had been nothing of any importance in that line would not necessarily be apparent to him, and she hoped he would get the picture – that she had not spent the whole of the past two and a half years pining for *him*!

Jonas was unusually silent, listening to her chatter without comment, his thick lashes veiling his eyes so that she was totally unaware of the effect her conversation was having.

After breakfast, Julie was introduced to Rob Macpherson for the first time.

When the meal was over, Jonas rose to his feet and said: 'Get your coat, Julie. I want to have a word with Rob before we leave.'

Julie, who had exhausted herself by talking throughout breakfast, felt vaguely resentful at the lack of response she had aroused. 'I trust he finds it easier to talk to you than I do,' she observed sarcastically.

Jonas walked to the door. He was wearing a thick cream sweater and black suede pants that clung to the muscles of his thighs as he moved, and Julie felt her senses stirring just looking at him. However, when he spoke he banished her weakness.

'When you have something interesting to say, I'll respond, Julie.'

Julie stared angrily at him. 'I thought my conversation would have interested you!'

'What? Women's magazines?' He shook his head. 'I don't think so.'

'It wasn't only that—'

The heavy-lidded eyes surveyed her mockingly. 'No, I agree. But the rest wasn't worth mentioning.'

Julie's coffee cup clattered into its saucer. 'You are rude, do you know that?'

'It's what comes of living alone so much,' he remarked tauntingly, and left the room.

Julie collected her sheepskin coat and went downstairs again. Following her instincts, she went along the corridor that led through the main part of the building. Half-way along, double doors gave on to an enormous banqueting hall, and as the doors were open Julie couldn't resist peering in.

The hall was well lit, with long windows overlooking the loch. Massive chandeliers were suspended from an enormously high ceiling overshadowing a long refectory table placed at one end. The walls were hung with tapestries, worn by the passage of years, and the floor which had once been polished now had a scuffed appearance. And yet for all that, there was an air of faded elegance about the place that Julie's artistic sensitivities responded to.

Leaving the hall, she continued past other doors, closed against her curiosity, and eventually reached the semi-circular hall of the other tower. She was looking about her uncertainly when Mrs Macpherson appeared down the stairs.

'Are you looking for Mr. Hunter, Mrs. Hunter?' she asked, with a smile.

Julie nodded. 'Yes. I hope you don't mind. I've been doing a bit of exploring for myself.'

'I? Mind?' Mrs. Macpherson clearly thought this was a strange thing for the wife of the master of the house to say, and she shook her head. 'When you come back, perhaps you'd like to see the rest of the castle.'

'Perhaps.' Julie was non-committal. 'Where is — my — my husband?'

'Come with me.' Mrs. Macpherson opened a door at the back of the hall. 'These rooms are Rob's and mine. Mrs. Drummond gave us our own apartments in this tower.'

'I see.' Julie looked about her with interest. 'It's very pleasant, isn't it?'

They passed through a comfortable living-room and now Julie could see that an extension jutted out from the tower at this point. Here Mrs. Macpherson had her kitchen, and beyond there were outbuildings and a yard. As they reached the kitchen, Julie could hear men's voices outside and presently a pair of spaniels came bounding into the house, attracted by the sound of their footsteps on the tiled floor of the kitchen.

'Och, get down, both of you!' exclaimed Mrs. Macpherson as they fussed about them, but Julie went down on her haunches, saying:

'Aren't they gorgeous! What are their names?'

'MacGregor and Macduff,' answered a strange voice, and looking up she saw that Jonas and another man had entered the kitchen after the animals. She guessed this was Rob Macpherson, although as far as she could see he appeared to have two perfectly normal legs. He was tall, too, almost as tall as Jonas, but broader, with iron grey hair, and a cheerfully weathered countenance.

Julie straightened and smiled. 'You must be Rob,' she said.

'That's right, Mrs. Hunter.' Rob shook hands with her warmly. Then he looked over his shoulder at Jonas. 'She's a fine bonny lass, isn't she? I'm surprised you permit her to live in that dreadful place without you.'

Julie flushed and Jonas's lips twitched. 'He means London, Julie. The Macphersons don't approve of modern – thinking.'

Julie ignored him. 'I was just admiring your dogs, Rob.'

'Ay, well, they're not my dogs,' replied Rob, shaking his head. 'They're your husband's. Didn't he tell you?'

Julie bit her lip. 'He – he wouldn't. He probably thought I'd disapprove. I – we never had any pets in London.'

'Not of the four-legged variety anyway,' commented Jonas annoyingly, and she badly wanted to wipe that mockery from his face.

'You'd know all about that, of course,' she retorted, her eyes flashing, and saw the shocked look that passed between Mrs. Macpherson and her husband. Oh, well, she thought irritably, he couldn't have it all his own way.

'I think we'd better go,' said Jonas, fastening the buttons of the brown leather coat he had put on over his sweater. Are you ready?'

Julie nodded, thrusting her hands into her coat pockets, and with a smile Jonas indicated that she should precede him outside. The dogs came after them, but at a command from Jonas they halted obediently, only their eyes eloquent of what they thought at being left behind.

They walked along the path that led to the steps, leaving the courtyard of the castle behind. Jonas had his injured hand in his pocket and Julie wondered guiltily whether she ought to have thanked Rob for his ministrations the night before.

Jonas was saying nothing, and with a sigh she exclaimed: 'You can't expect me to put up with your disparaging comments all the time!'

Jonas went ahead of her down the steps. 'You've lost your sense of humour, Julie.'

'*I've* lost *my* sense of humour!' she echoed indignantly.

'That's what I said.'

'I know what you said. I said. I just don't happen to see any humour in this situation.'

'Oh, there is, believe me.' He glanced round at her, but there didn't seem to be any amusement in his set features and she hunched her shoulders resentfully.

'Why is it you always try to make me feel the guilty party?' she demanded.

'Perhaps because you are,' he responded coolly, and she determined to say nothing more unless he did.

He was able to start the outboard motor with his left hand although it was obviously a handicap, and watching him Julie felt sick at heart. But she huddled in her seat and stared out across the water, silently justifying her attitude.

The sky was much higher this morning and there were occasional breaks in the cloud allowing glimpses of the blue sky above. But the hills were still shrouded in mist, and there was an icy chill in the breeze that blew across from the mainland. The loch lay tranquil within its surrounding belt of firs, blue-grey in places, and utterly enchanting. Even Julie found herself responding to its natural beauty.

Jonas propelled the boat down the shingle and jumped

aboard as it drifted on the swell. They moved smoothly out into the centre of the loch, rocking a little as the breeze caught them. Julie stared ahead, seeing the jetty where Jonas had garaged the car, and feeling a slight sense of excitement at the prospect of driving such a powerful vehicle. But the reasons why she was to drive him to Newton Carn brought a recollection that momentarily destroyed her determination to remain silent.

'You said Rob had only one leg!' she exclaimed, turning to look at Jonas.

Jonas raised dark eyebrows. 'So?'

'He appears to have two.'

Jonas looked bored. 'Haven't you heard of artificial limbs?'

Julie flushed. 'Are you sure that's what it is? How does he manage to get up and down all those steps?'

'What a suspicious mind you have, Julie,' remarked Jonas, with dislike. 'How do you think he gets up and down? He walks. He manages. I expect he's glad of the exercise.'

Julie looked down at her hands, warmly encased in sheepskin gloves. 'If I'm suspicious, you have only yourself to blame,' she mumbled.

Jonas gave a short laugh. 'Oh, yes, I know. You have made that point blatantly clear.'

He tied the boat up at the jetty, vaulting on to its concrete surface and offering his hand to Julie. She avoided it, climbing out of the boat unaided, and waiting impatiently while he unlocked the garage doors. She looked up the road towards Achnacraig. How far was it? Four miles? Five? How long would it take her to walk that far? One hour – two? She sighed. There would be a train to Inverness that afternoon. Why didn't she just abandon this expedition and get on it before something disastrous happened?

She became suddenly aware that Jonas was standing watching her. His lean face was dark and brooding and the car keys were dangling from the fingers of his uninjured hand.

'You can use the car, if you like,' he offered quietly.

She started. 'What do you mean?'

'To drive to Achnacraig. That was what you were thinking, wasn't it?'

Julie stamped her feet to warm them. 'It's cold. Shall we get going?'

Jonas looked at her strangely. 'I won't stop you, you know.'

Julie brushed past him, snatching the car keys from his hand. 'I said I would drive you to Newton Carn, and I will,' she retorted, going into the garage.

The powerful sports saloon started at a touch and she reversed it carefully out of the garage. Jonas closed the garage doors and then climbed into the squab seat beside her.

'You'd better put on the safety harness,' he commented, putting an arm behind her to indicate the straps. 'Do you understand the gears?'

Julie looked down. 'I think so. I – I've driven one of these before, haven't I?'

'You have. This the third Porsche I've owned.'

'Hmm.' Julie nodded. 'How fast will it go?'

Jonas adjusted his clothes more comfortably. 'I won't tell you what I've had on the clock. I don't want to terrify you.'

Julie half smiled, and with a lightening of her spirits she swung out on to the road, turning left at Jonas's instigation for Newton Carn.

The road to Newton Carn was rather hair-raising in

places in its own right without the added complication of a car that behaved rather like a leashed tiger at times, purring at high speeds and snarling a little when subdued to a steady forty. The scenery was quite spectacular. Much of the road ran between lochs on narrow peninsulas of land, edged with reeds. She was glad they met nothing on the journey except a farm cart which was quite prepared to move aside for them. She doubted her ability to reverse the Porsche on such narrow roads without ending up in the loch.

They saw some of the aggressively horned Highland cattle grazing among the heather and once a deer dashed across the road ahead of them. That incident almost unnerved Julie and she was glad when Jonas said: 'Stop for a few minutes. There's no hurry.'

She brought the car to a halt on a rough lip of land jutting into the loch, leaving the road clear in case any other vehicle did happen this way. Jonas took out his cheroots, rolled down his window, and lit one. Julie wished she smoked. She would have liked to have had something to calm her nerves just then. Resting her hands on the steering wheel, she said: 'Tell me about South America.'

Jonas exhaled lazily. 'What do you want to know?'

'Where did you live? What did you do? What were the people like?'

He slid lower in his seat, raising one foot to rest carelessly against the dashboard, his head against the soft leather upholstery. 'That's quite a question.'

Julie looked down at his bandaged hand resting on his thigh. 'Don't you want to tell me?'

'Don't start that again!' Jonas sounded impatient. Then he sighed. 'Okay, I lived in Maracaibo for a time before moving on to Rio and Buenos Aires.' He inhaled on his cheroot. 'I enjoyed the work, actually. And the people are very friendly.'

'I see.' Julie digested this, not without a twinge of envy.

Jonas looked sideways at her. 'What did you expect me to say? Work is the ideal panacea.'

Julie ignored this. 'Did – did you get to know many people?'

Jonas's face hardened. 'Women, you mean?'

Julie shook her head. 'I didn't say that.'

'No. But the implication was there. Sure, I got to know a lot of people – women as well as men. South American women are quite something.'

She had asked for that, but it didn't make it any the less painful. She turned her head and looked through the window. Several birds were wheeling in the air above their heads, swooping and diving towards the loch with effortless grace.

'Tell me about you,' Jonas said unexpectedly, and her head jerked round.

'I told you about me at breakfast,' she replied.

'No, you didn't. You talked a lot of nonsense about parties and deadlines and the men you've been mixing with. I want to hear about the real you, your personal life, what you've been doing – about this flat you rent in Pallister Court.'

Julie gasped. 'How do you know I rent a flat in Pallister Court?'

Jonas shook his head. 'Do you see much of Angela these days?'

Julie's fingers curved tightly round the steering wheel. 'As a matter of fact, she's sharing the flat at the moment,' she admitted reluctantly.

'Is she?' Jonas didn't sound surprised. 'And how did

that come about?'

'The building where she had her flat was pulled down to make way for a new block.'

'Didn't they offer her alternative accommodation?'

'Actually, they did. But she didn't want to live in one of those glass and concrete structures. Pallister Court is old, but it's attractive.'

Jonas's mouth turned down at the corners. 'I'm sure it is. So how long is she staying?'

Julie shrugged. 'I don't know. Does it matter?'

'To me, yes.' He thrust himself up in his seat, his eyes hard and uncompromising. 'Let's go!'

Julie started the engine obediently, but she was disturbed by his behaviour. She knew that Angela had never liked Jonas, but she had never before realized exactly how much Jonas disliked Angela. Still, she argued reasonably, it was natural that whatever feelings he had felt for her would be destroyed when she had betrayed his unfaithfulness, unable, as he had been, to deceive his wife.

The pain this memory evoked caused Julie to press her foot hard down on the accelerator, and the Porsche fairly jumped forward, so that Jonas said: 'Death wish?' as they approached a corner at speed.

Julie relaxed the pressure at once and applied the brakes, controlling the skid that could have overturned them, only to find she was trembling. She stopped the car and rested her hot forehead against the cool surface of the steering wheel. 'I'm sorry,' she muttered, ashamed of her emotionalism. 'I – I'm not used to having such power under the bonnet.'

She felt the familiar sense of having behaved stupidly assail her. She had been over it all a hundred times in her mind. Why did she persist in letting memories tear her apart? Was it because the idea of any other woman sharing the intimacies she had shared with Jonas filled her with a sick sense of despair, or was it made worse because she had heard the other woman's side of it, too? Angela had wanted to exonerate herself – in the circumstances that was natural – and Julie had been placed in the impossible position of having to forgive her friend for something that had been wholly her husband's fault.

'Stop indulging yourself!'

Jonas's words were harsh and cruel, and she lifted her head to look at him. 'Indulging myself? How?'

'Self-pity is a form of self-indulgence. Don't pretend you're not feeling sorry for yourself, because I don't believe it.'

His words had a sobering effect as she guessed he had intended they should have, and with a determined effort she wiped her moist palms down the seams of her pants and licking her lips put the car back into gear again.

It didn't take much longer to reach Newton Carn and as they drove along the village street, Julie looked about her with interest. There was the usual cluster of cottages, a store which appeared to sell everything imaginable, with a small café attached, a chapel and schoolhouse, and a few larger dwellings. It was to one of these larger houses that Jonas directed her, and as they turned between stone gate posts she saw the doctor's plate beside the door.

'Will you wait in the car?' he inquired, thrusting open his door and getting out.

Julie looked across at him. 'Will you be long?'

He shrugged. 'That depends. The doctor might not be here, in which case I would have to wait.'

Julie sighed. 'I think I'd rather go for a walk. If you have no objections.'

'None at all.' He straightened. 'If I'm ready before you

get back, I'll wait in the car.'

He was cool and she wished she could do something to restore the relationship they had had before he started asking questions about Angela. He was walking towards the entrance, and she pushed open her door and scrambled out.

'Jonas—'

He turned, his hard handsome face uncompromising. 'Yes?'

She faltered, 'W-would you like me to come with you?'

'Where? To see the doctor? I think not.'

He turned to the door again and she covered the space between them in seconds. 'Jonas, I'd like to . . .'

He looked down at her. 'Why?'

She shrugged, moving uncomfortably. 'Oh – just, because . . .' She sighed. 'Couldn't we be friends?'

His lips twisted. 'You have too many friends already, Julie,' he retorted coldly, and opened the door and entered the doctor's house.

Julie stood where he had left her feeling unaccountably chilled. Then she hunched her shoulders, thrust her hands into her pockets, and walked slowly back to the car. She locked the doors, pocketed the keys, and after another fleeting glance at the house she walked to the gate.

There were few people about in the village, and those that there were looked at her a trifle curiously, obviously wondering who she was and where she had come from. She walked to the end of the village street and stopped by a gate leading into some pastureland. There were a few sheep grazing, but the grass was crisp and frosty and the trees that were not conifers looked stark and skeletal without their leaves. She leaned on the gate, her elbows resting on the top bar, her chin cupped in her hands. She still felt ridiculously emotional and she forced herself to think of the interview which had brought her here.

It wouldn't be difficult to write about Jonas. She already knew enough about him to fill a book, but they were not the sort of things she could, or even wanted to, write down. However, if she kept the article on an impersonal footing she could use his general background, education, etc., to create a word picture of him. Maybe he would tell her a little more about the work he had done in South America, and she guessed that having achieved success with one book he would most certainly write another.

She was lost in thought when a hand descended on her shoulder and she swung round in surprise to find Jonas just behind her.

'I – I thought you were going to wait in the car,' she stammered.

'You have the keys,' he pointed out dryly. 'Besides, I enjoyed the walk.' He looked towards the mountains which seemed so much closer here without the reflective expanse of water between them. 'It's a pleasant morning.'

He moved away from her and she gathered her composure. 'Did – did you see the doctor?'

'MacTavish? Yes, I saw him.'

'So? What did he say?'

'It's nothing serious. So far as he can ascertain, Rob got all the glass out. He's put a couple of stitches in my palm, that's all.'

Julie felt relieved. 'Thank goodness for that!'

'Why? What's it to you?' His eyes were dark and contemptuous. 'Are you afraid I might ask you to stay even longer to act as my secretary?'

Julie bent her head. 'Shall we go back to the castle?'

'If you like.' He was indifferent.

Julie scuffed her toe. 'It's only half past ten. Do you want to buy me a cup of coffee?'

Jonas had begun to walk back along the village street, but now he turned and frowned. 'Coffee? Where?'

'The café. It's open, isn't it?'

'I suppose so.'

'There you are, then.'

'Very well.' He waited for her to catch up with him. 'But I should have thought you'd have realized that if we go straight back to Castle Lochcraig you can get the interview over and catch the afternoon train to Inverness!'

Julie caught her breath. 'What's the matter with you?' she exclaimed. 'What have I done that has annoyed you so much? Why are you being so – so objectionable?'

'Objectionable?' He looked at her strangely. 'I thought you were eager to leave.'

Julie's cheeks suffused with colour. 'All right, all right. We'll go straight back to Castle Lochcraig as you say. I'll interview you this morning, and I'll leave this afternoon.'

She set away running, running back to where the car was still standing in the drive of Doctor MacTavish's house. Jonas caught her easily, halting her with his unbandaged hand, bringing her up short.

'The café's over here,' he said, and something in his voice stopped her from contradicting him. 'Let's have that coffee.'

While the elderly woman who ran the little snack bar attended to their needs, Jonas told her about a restaurant he had discovered in Caracas, Venezuela's capital, where the steaks were the thickest he had ever seen. They were served, he said, with jacket potatoes dressed with sour cream, and the way he described it Julie could almost taste them. Jonas had always had this tremendous gift for description. The casual conversation relaxed her so that she was emboldened to ask:

'Why did you decide to write a novel?'

Jonas lit a cheroot, exhaling the aromatic smoke into the air around them. 'I wanted to try something new,' he replied slowly. 'I was sick of living in foreign countries. I wanted to come back to England.'

Julie didn't ask the most obvious question, avoiding the pitfalls that would open up. 'And do you intend to write another? Novel, I mean.'

Jonas considered the coffee in his cup. 'Oh, yes, I'll write another. I already have it mapped out.'

'How exciting!' Julie wasn't feigning her enthusiasm. 'What is it to be about?'

'It's another – what you would call – political thriller. It's set in a Central American republic. Something I have first-hand knowledge about.'

Julie put down her cup and rested her chin on her hands. 'You always wanted to write fiction, didn't you?'

'Umm, of a kind. My fiction tends to be closely allied to fact.'

'Do you remember when you wrote that terribly torrid espionage story with a sort of James Bond type hero?' She chuckled. 'I said at the time you should have sent it to a publisher. They'd have loved it. It had everything – sex, violence, a good story line. But you didn't want to ruin your reputation as a serious journalist!'

Jonas's eyes held hers. 'I only did it because you asked me to,' he said quietly.

Julie dragged her face away from his. 'Do you – do you

still have the manuscript?'

'Yes.' He paused. 'Do you want to see it?'

Julie's breathing was suddenly constricted. 'I – no! I don't think so.'

He inclined his head and with a shrug finished his coffee. 'Shall we go?'

It seemed cooler when they emerged from the café and Julie shivered, drawing her coat closer about her. The sun was now hidden by a heavy belt of clouds and the freshness of the morning was disappearing beneath a thickening pall of mist. Jonas looked up at the sky and frowned.

'I think we'd better get back to the castle as quickly as possible,' he essayed thoughtfully. 'I shouldn't like you to have to drive these roads without being able to see any more than a few yards ahead of you.'

It was really thick by the time they reached the jetty. Julie garaged the car and Jonas locked the garage. Then they both climbed into the boat.

'Let me pull the motor,' she suggested anxiously, noticing that for all he had dismissed his injuries as being of little account, there were definite lines of strain beside his mouth.

Jonas shook his head. 'I can do it. As you said earlier, I'm not completely helpless.'

Julie was glad when they reached the island for more reasons than one. The dampness was more chilling than rain and as they mounted the steps to the castle she drew the hood of her coat over her head. They entered the building through the tower entrance they had used two days before, but Mrs. Macpherson must have seen them coming because she met them in the hall. She looked at Jonas with evident concern, her gaze barely flickering over Julie before she exclaimed: 'You look worn out, Mr.

Hunter. Did you not see Doctor MacTavish?'

'Oh yes, I saw him,' replied Jonas, removing his leather coat with some difficulty so that the housekeeper clicked her tongue and hurried forward to assist him. 'He's given me some antibiotics in case of infection, but he said that Rob had made an excellent job of cleaning me up.'

Julie glanced quickly at him. Wasn't he going to mention the stitches the doctor had put in his palm?

Mrs. Macpherson folded his coat over her arm. 'Well, you go into the living-room, sir, and get warm. I'll bring along some coffee in five minutes.'

'No – really, no, thank you, Mrs. Macpherson.' Jonas shook his head. 'We – er – we had coffee in Newton Carn.'

'Where? At the doctor's?'

'No. At a café,' put in Julie, becoming impatient at her obvious exclusion from the conversation. 'It was very nice.'

Mrs. Macpherson looked disapproving. 'You went to Annie Macdonald's?' she exclaimed.

'If that was her name, yes—'

'Mrs. Hunter was thirsty,' commented Jonas, with a sigh. 'How long will lunch be?'

The housekeeper's features were stiff. 'Whenever you say. Fifteen minutes – half an hour.'

'Fifteen minutes will be fine,' agreed Jonas, and turned to Julie as she was struggling out of her coat. But she moved away so that he could not help her and dropped the coat carelessly on to a carved chair that stood against the wall. Then she preceded him into the living-room, leaving Mrs. Macpherson to go and attend to the meal.

'What was that all about?' Julie demanded as soon as the door was closed.

Jonas went to help himself to a drink. 'Feuds, vendettas. Who knows?' He swallowed some Scotch and half turned. 'No, actually, Annie Dalrymple, as she was called before her marriage, used to be Rob's sweetheart. Then she married Hugh Macdonald and Rob married Ellen.'

'Ellen – Ellen MacPherson, I suppose you mean?'

'Ellen Stuart as she was then.'

Julie shook her head. 'She certainly thinks a lot about you.'

Jonas turned away to finish pouring more Scotch. 'Jealous?'

Julie ignored this. 'Should you be drinking so much when you're taking drugs?'

'I'm taking antibiotics,' he corrected her dryly.

'Antibiotics are drugs!'

'Technically I suppose they are. But they're not narcotics, which is what I believe you're talking about.' He raised his glass. 'Do you want a drink?'

'No.' She moved her shoulders irritably. 'You have to be right, don't you? Anyway, you are drinking too much. It's only half past twelve!'

'Am I to answer to you for my actions?' he queried tautly.

'No. No, of course not. I'm only thinking of your well-being.' She moved restlessly about the room. 'As Mrs. Macpherson said, you look worn out. Why don't you rest?'

'I thought you wanted an interview. If I go to bed, I may sleep for the rest of the day.'

Julie stared at him. 'I don't believe you did sleep well last night, did you? Why did you say you had?'

Jonas flung himself into one of the comfortable armchairs. 'Julie, why don't you mind your own business, hmm?'

Julie folded her arms across her body, pressing her

95

palms to her elbows. 'I'm not a machine, Jonas. If you're tired, you should rest.' She looked at his bandaged hand lying on the arm of the chair. 'Does it hurt much? Your hand, I mean?'

He closed his eyes resignedly. 'Julie, it was my own fault. Stop feeling so guilty. You have nothing to reproach yourself with.'

Julie stared down at him frustratedly. 'I know I haven't!' she burst out impatiently. 'But if I hadn't come here . . .' She turned away. 'Oh, I'm going up to my room. I – I need to use the bathroom.'

When she came downstairs again, Mrs. Macpherson was waiting for her in the hall. The door to the living-room was closed and the housekeeper raised a silencing finger to her lips.

'Mr. Hunter is asleep,' she whispered. 'Come along to the dining-room. I'll serve your lunch and keep Mr. Hunter's hot for later.'

Julie complied, looking back rather regretfully at the closed door. She would have liked to have seen Jonas asleep . . . and vulnerable.

CHAPTER SIX

AFTER another of Mrs. Macpherson's satisfying meals, Julie left the dining-room and walked back to the tower hallway. The door to the living-room was still closed and she pressed her ear against the panels, hoping to hear some sound from within. But either Jonas was still sleeping or the panels were too thick, because she couldn't hear anything at all.

Sighing, she turned away. If he had slept badly the night before, she ought not to wake him. He was bound to be tired after the amount of blood he had lost, and she ought to be glad he was recovering his strength. All the same, the time left to her to talk to him – to really talk to him, that was – was dwindling.

She went up the stairs to the gallery. Through the narrow windows there was little to be seen. The mist had thickened and shrouded the edges of the loch, isolating them in a world of grey dampness and swirling cloud. She shivered. She was glad she was not having to venture out in that again today.

She looked up the stairs that disappeared to some unknown region above her head. She was curious to know where they led, and feeling strangely loath to spend a lonely hour in her room, she began to climb. She did not have to go far before she encountered a stout wooden door, locked and bolted against her. The keys were in the lock, however, and the bolt creaked but moved without too much difficulty. Feeling an intense sense of anticipation, she pushed the door forward and then gasped as the cold air from outside the castle swept in on her.

She was on the battlements, she realized belatedly, grasping the stone parapet to steady herself. Although the wind was not strong yet it was cold, having brought the mist down from the icy reaches of the mountains and it caught her breath. She pressed a protective hand to her throat. She could imagine how delightful it must be up here in the height of summer, but there was little pleasure there on this chill October afternoon. All that was visible were the turreted outcrops of the parapet, and even they looked unreal looming out of the smoky gloom. She was more than willing to step inside again and close the heavy door against the elements.

When the key had been turned and the bolt fastened, she went down to the gallery again. The fire burning in her bedroom was very welcome and not until she had toasted herself for several minutes did she stop shivering. Even so, she had to admit, the castle was a fascinating old place, and in other circumstances she would have enjoyed studying its history. It was always amazing to consider how long these primitively designed structures had stood up to the force of the elements, and she wondered with a morbid curiosity whether its history contained any records of anyone throwing themselves from the battlements on to the jagged rocks below.

She pushed such unpleasant thoughts aside and determinedly picked up her briefcase. She extracted the file on Jonas and flicking it open tried to summon enthusiasm for her task. The queries she had penned mocked her. She was no nearer having them answered now than when she arrived.

Putting the file aside, she went over to her suitcase and opened it. The few things she had brought were soon packed, leaving only her night things and toiletries to be added in the morning. She felt better after that. She had made some move towards leaving and she felt less frustrated at her enforced delay. Only her blouse and suit remained to be returned to her, and as she would be wearing them when she left . . .

She straightened and looked towards the wardrobe that contained all those clothes. On impulse, she opened the wardrobe door and ran her fingers lightly over the soft materials. Silks, chiffons, jerseys – who did they belong to? Such brilliant colours, such beautiful garments. Who had Jonas had in mind when he bought them? Not *her*, surely? And yet the more she thought about it, the more doubtful she became. Why else were they here? He couldn't have done it to humiliate her, not when he had introduced her to the Macphersons as his wife, when he had gone out of his way to convince them that they were a happily married couple. And if the Macphersons were scandalized at the idea of divorce, he would hardly be likely to bring some other woman here to stay with him, would he?

She closed the door again and looked down at the green corded pants she was wearing. They did fit her, and the fact that they were a little loose pointed to the fact of his remembering her as she had been before . . . before . . .

She drew a trembling breath. No! It couldn't be true. He couldn't have bought these things with the intention of luring her here and keeping her, could he? How did he propose to accomplish such a thing? If that had been his intention, how were the Macphersons expected to react?

She licked dry lips. Calm down, she told herself, for the umpteenth time since she had arrived. You're jumping to conclusions! But they were not unreasonable conclusions, she argued urgently. And she had been here three days already!

She paced uneasily about the bedroom. What if she was right? What if everything she had supposed was true? He was a clever man, she had never doubted that. He was not likely to choose some violent method to keep her here. It was much more characteristic that he should detain her on a voluntary basis. Like the injury to his hand, for example. He had not asked her to drive him to Newton Carn, he was too clever for that. She had offered — *as he had gambled she would*! And if tomorrow his hand was still causing him pain, might she feel obliged to stay a few more days?

Anxiety gave way to anger. What were his plans? What were his ultimate intentions? Why had he brought her here? To arouse her sympathy? Her compassion? To weaken her resistance against him? And if so, why? Why should he want that — why should he want *her*, in any capacity? Because she had walked out on him. Because she had refused to be placated by his facile explanations? Had that piqued him? That she should walk out on him? Before he was ready to walk out on her? He had always been attractive to women, she had accepted that. Was his ego such that he needed to satisfy himself that he could make a slave of her again before abandoning her?

Her fists clenched and unclenched and then clenched again. There had to be some truth there somewhere. And she was making it so easy for him! That was the galling part. That was what brought the bitter bile of resentment to her throat. She ignored the ache her suspicions aroused in her heart and hardened her resolve. How could she have been such a fool? He might almost have succeeded in duping her again. But this time he had been just a little too clever!

The darkening skies brought her to awareness of the

lateness of the hour. It was after four o'clock and although the firelit room was attractive it was also eerily remote, and in Julie's morose frame of mind she needed lights and activity. Collecting her briefcase, she left the room and went along the gallery and down the spiral staircase. She would speak to Jonas now, this minute, she would tell him she was leaving first thing in the morning and if he refused her the interview, then that was just too bad.

She opened the living-room door without ceremony and then halted, her determination momentarily failing. Jonas was stretched out on the couch, the glow from the fading fire illuminating the darkness of his lashes resting against his cheekbones, the hollows below and the softened curve of his thin mouth. One arm was supporting his head while his injured hand lay limply against his thigh.

Julie stared at him impatiently. Was he really asleep or had he heard her opening the door and feigned unconsciousness? She couldn't be sure and in her mood she decided she didn't much care. Either way, she was determined to arouse him, and she entered the room and closed the door with a heavy thud.

Jonas's eyes flickered open at once. A frown drew his brows together and he blinked and propped himself up on one elbow, staring at her almost blankly. If he hadn't been asleep he was certainly making damn good pretence of it, thought Julie uncharitably, and she moved out of the shadows saying: 'If you'll tell me how, I'll light the lamps.'

Jonas expelled his breath on a sigh and slumped back on the couch. 'Use a taper. Turn on the gas tap and hold the taper to the top of the mantel. It will ignite almost immediately.'

Julie reached for a taper and followed his directions. She lighted all the lamps around the walls so that the room was soon quite brightly illuminated. Then she threw the used taper into the fire and turned to the couch, a resolute expression on her face.

'I hate to bring this up,' she began, not without some sarcasm, 'but we do have an interview to conduct. If you feel up to it, I'd like to get on with it right away.'

Jonas swung his legs to the floor and ran a hand round the back of his neck, flexing his stiff muscles. 'I need a drink,' he said, not answering her. 'Have you had lunch?'

'Have I had lunch?' Julie stifled an angry retort. 'Of course, I've had lunch. It's nearly half past four.'

'Is it?' He glanced halfheartedly at his watch. 'Hmm, so it is. I must have slept for quite a while.'

'You have.' Julie controlled her temper with difficulty. 'You were tired.'

He nodded, the dark eyes steadily gaining in penetration. 'What have you been doing? Going through the papers in my study?'

'No!' Julie was indignant, but her cheeks flushed. 'I've been upstairs. In my room.'

He yawned and gave an apologetic shake of his head. 'Hmm, well – I'm hungry.' He looked up at her. 'Ask Mrs. Macpherson to make me a sandwich, would you, Julie?'

'Ask her yourself!' Julie's mouth was mutinous. 'I'm not your servant!'

His eyes widened. 'I see.' They narrowed. 'What is it, Julie? What am I supposed to have done now?'

'What haven't you done?' Julie was finding it extremely hard not to become emotional over this. 'Look, Jonas, I've been thinking—'

'Ah, so that's it!'

His voice was mocking and she longed to be able to hurt him as he had hurt her. 'As I said,' she continued tautly, 'I've been thinking, and I've come to the conclusion that your intention all along has been to keep me here.'

'Oh, really?' Jonas stretched his long legs in front of him. 'Why should I want to do that?'

'I – I don't really know,' Julie sighed.

'You didn't have to come,' he pointed out dryly.

'No – no, I know that. But you must have known I would.'

'Did I?'

'You said you knew Mark Bernstein.'

'I know *of* him.'

'All right, then. You must have known he wouldn't pass up the opportunity to interview the man whose book is presently topping the best-seller lists both here and in the United States!'

'I thought it would interest him.'

Julie opened her mouth to speak and then closed it again as what he had said registered. '*You* thought it would interest him,' she echoed disbelievingly. 'You mean – you mean – you *offered* him the interview?'

Jonas's eyes were disturbingly intent. 'I offered it to *you*, Julie.'

'Then – then it was you who told Mark of our relationship, that I was still your wife?' She could scarcely believe it.

'That's right. Well, you are, aren't you?'

'Technically, perhaps.' Julie licked dry lips. 'But not for much longer. I want a divorce, Jonas.'

'Do you?'

'Yes.' She brushed a dazed hand across her forehead.

'Jonas – why? Why? Why did you bring me here?'

'I should have thought you'd have figured that out too. I wanted to talk to you – to explain—'

'Oh, *no*!' Julie moved her head helplessly from side to side. 'I don't want to hear any more explanations—'

'Nevertheless, you are going to.' Jonas rose to his feet and she unconsciously moved back from him. 'In the beginning I was too sick with the whole filthy business to care one way or the other. But in South America I had plenty of time to think, and when I got back from there and found that you and Angela had set up house together—' He broke off, his expression grim. 'Julie, listen to me! I did not – ever – make love to Angela or any other woman after we were married!'

Julie flinched. 'Please, Jonas, don't bring that up again! I – I've told you – it's over, finished! I don't want to talk about it.'

'Damn you, don't you?' His hand shot out, encircling her upper arm, drawing her closer to him so that she could feel the warmth of his breath on her forehead. 'But I do. Surely I have the right to a hearing.'

Julie's breathing felt constricted and she was supremely conscious of the cruelty of those fingers encircling her arm. 'Jonas, nothing you can say can alter the fact that Angela slept at the apartment!'

'I don't deny that.'

'And that – and that she was – in our bed—'

'Yes, but *I* was not!' he snapped harshly.

'You had been.'

'That's Angela's story.'

'Oh, Jonas!' Julie felt the familiar feeling of sickness she always felt whenever she considered the intimate aspects of the affair. 'Jonas, don't – please bring that all up again. I – I can't stand it.'

Jonas's mouth was hard. 'I have had to stand it for over two years, Julie.'

'You – you shouldn't have – have done – what you did.'

'God help me, I didn't do anything!' He raked his bandaged hand over his thick hair. 'God, why won't you believe me? Why do you persist in believing Angela's story? Can't you see it was a fabrication? Haven't you the sense to realize she was always jealous of us?'

Julie stood with her head bent, waiting for him to release her. She felt sick and empty, filled with dread and despair. She had known that sooner or later it would come to this, but she still wasn't prepared for the agony of it all.

With an ugly imprecation Jonas released her, pushing her aside so roughly that she almost fell. 'All right,' he muttered coldly, 'so whatever I say you won't believe me, is that it?'

'Jonas,' she began, choosing her words with care, 'Jonas, I didn't come here for personal reasons. You know that. What's between us – well, it's useless trying to take up old grievances. We – we each have our own lives now. You can't deny you've achieved more success since we split up than ever you did when we were living together.'

'I had other – distractions then,' he said bleakly. 'Work was not the whole of my existence as it is now.'

'Oh, Jonas, I can't believe you devote the whole of your time to your work,' she exclaimed, trying to introduce a lighter note. 'I – I mean, you have friends. Both male and female.'

'Yes?' His lips twisted. 'That's what you think, is it? Does it help to salve your conscience?'

'What do you mean?'

'Well, it was pretty easy to shrug me off, wasn't it?'

'Shrug you off—?'

'Yes. Pretty easy to pretend disbelief of anything I said because it suited you to do so.'

'That's not true, Jonas.' Julie's face was strained now. 'Oh, God, all right – all right, let's discuss it. Let's go through all the sordid details. Let me think now – how did it happen? I'd been away, hadn't I? I was working on that story for the *Herald* and I had had to go up to Lincolnshire, hadn't I? I was away overnight and wasn't expected back until later in the day. But the job folded and I got back soon after seven a.m. And what did I find? Surprise, surprise! My husband shaving in the bathroom and my best friend naked in our bed!' Her voice almost broke, but she controlled it. 'Now – now, I was generous and asked what was going on. What could be going on? Angela's apartment was only about a mile away across town, so she could hardly have found it impossible to get home, could she? So what other reason could there be for her staying there—'

'I told you, Julie. She came to the apartment stoned out of her mind!'

Julie's eyes flashed. 'Angela doesn't get drunk!'

'She did that night. To give her courage, perhaps?'

'Jonas, stop it! You know you're lying. Angela told me what happened. God, how she told me! Rushing out of bed to me, begging me to forgive her, imploring me to believe that she hadn't been to blame, that you'd taken her to dinner and given her so much to drink that she didn't know what she was doing—'

'For God's sake, I did not take Angela to dinner!' he bit out, through his teeth. 'Why the hell should I take that bitch to dinner? You know I never liked her—'

'You mean she didn't like you.'

'Angela doesn't like *you*, or hadn't you realized?'

Julie gasped. 'That's a foul thing to say!'

'This is a foul business. Aren't I allowed to defend myself?'

'Oh, Jonas, please, must we go on?'

'Yes, we must.' His jaw was taut. 'You wouldn't listen to reason then, but by God! you're going to listen to reason now.'

'Your reason.'

'Yes, my reason.' Jonas raked his fingers through his hair. 'Julie, when I opened the apartment door and found Angela almost collapsing on the step, what was I supposed to do? Shove her away and leave her to any possible fate which might befall her? She was your friend – or so I thought. I knew what you would have done in the same circumstances, and I did it. I brought her in, I gave her black coffee, and when she passed out I laid her on our bed. God help me, Julie, that's all I did. I didn't take her clothes off, I didn't go to bed with her, and I sure as hell didn't make love to her!'

Julie's head was throbbing. She had heard Jonas's story before, but she still could not accept it. It was so unlikely. Angela was simply not that kind of girl. All right, she accepted to some extent that Angela distrusted men, but that was easily explained. Her father had run off with a girl very much younger than her mother when she was still at school and she had never forgiven him for that. But Julie had never known her drink a lot and to imagine her getting drunk and going to the apartment when she knew Julie was away seemed totally unacceptable. And then to pretend that Jonas had taken advantage of her? Oh, no, that was going much too far. Who did Jonas think he was fooling? Himself, possibly? But Angela was attractive to men, and considering the reputation he had

had before their marriage . . .

'Jonas, this is useless, can't you see? We're just going round and round in circles.' She drew an unsteady breath. 'I'm leaving in the morning, interview or no interview. I shall tell Mark exactly what has happened and I shall hope he believes me. If not, I don't expect I'll find it too difficult to get another job.'

Jonas walked across to the cabinet and poured himself a stiff Scotch. He threw the raw liquid to the back of his throat and then turned, leaning against the wall. 'All right, Julie,' he said, and there was a disturbingly defeated look in his eyes which unwillingly tore at her heart. 'Ask your questions. Don't be shy. I'd hate to be responsible for you losing your job as well as everything else.'

'But – but you haven't eaten—'

'I'm not hungry.' He poured another Scotch. 'Don't trouble yourself about me, Julie. I can do without your kind of sympathy.'

It was much later that evening that Julie sat beside the fire in her bedroom, looking through the sheaf of shorthand notes she had taken during her interview with Jonas. She was curiously loath to translate them into longhand. She had her own peculiar style of shorthand and so long as they remained only symbols on a scrap of paper only she could read them. She sighed. It had been the worst evening she had spent since she came here, although in fact it had been the quietest. Perhaps that was what had got through to her. The impersonality Jonas had so effectively generated after their confrontation. She thrust the papers aside and lay back in her chair. What was the matter with her? She had been angry and resentful at his attempts to create some kind of relationship between them, but now that he had abandoned any effort to be friendly she found she felt curiously drained. He had behaved like a stranger at dinner, and she had been chilled to the core of her being.

She rose from the chair and shedding her robe she turned out the lamps and climbed into the huge bed. The fire was dying, but it still cast a shadowy light over the room. She lay staring up at the carved ceiling. This was the last night she would spend in this bed, she thought, and wondered why the knowledge did not fill her with elation. She was leaving in the morning, that was definite now, so why did she feel this underlying sense of despair?

For the very first time since that terrible morning when she had returned to the apartment and found Angela there she allowed an element of doubt to enter her brain. What if – what if there was some truth in what Jonas said? What if each of their stories, Jonas's and Angela's, had an element of truth in them? What if Jonas had taken Angela to dinner, what if she had drunk too much and he had had to bring her back to the apartment? What if Angela had misconstrued his attentions?

But no! Julie swallowed convulsively. *No!* Angela had been very explicit. Destructively explicit! There had been no mistake on her part. So where did that leave them? In exactly the same position as they had been before Jonas's outburst. It was quite simple – either she believed Angela, or she believed Jonas. And quite honestly, Jonas's story was so unlikely that she had never seriously considered it. But what if she did? What if Angela was lying? What had she got to gain by it? And why would she go to the apartment while Julie was away? She had never appeared to like Jonas after they were married. Was it because she distrusted all attractive men after her father's behaviour?

Jonas's reputation could not have helped.

There still remained the fact that Angela *had* gone out with Jonas, if her story was to be believed. Hardly the behaviour of someone who despised her escort. If Jonas had invited her, though, perhaps she had not wanted to create open hostility between them by refusing.

Julie sighed and rolled on to her stomach. Perhaps she should have been sophisticated enough to forget what had happened. She knew that other of her friends' husbands had been unfaithful without an irretrievable breakdown of their marriages. Indeed, she even knew of women who were cheating on their husbands without too much conscience.

But she had never been like that; she had believed in the sanctity of marriage. She was old-fashioned, perhaps, but she had wanted no other woman's leftovers. Perhaps she ought not to have got married in this day and age when promiscuity was treated so lightly. Angela seemed to have a good time without tying herself down. But Julie hadn't considered it a penance. She had liked cooking, and even cleaning had its compensations. She had looked forward to the time when they would have children. She had wanted to feel Jonas's child moving in her. It was a disturbingly satisfying prospect. But that was all over now ...

A pain stirred in her stomach. It still hurt her, oh, God! How it hurt her. She had loved Jonas, really loved him. She would have done anything for him, anything ... Anything except accept his unfaithfulness ...

She must have fallen into an uneasy slumber because when she opened her eyes again the room was quite dark, the only illumination coming from outside through a crack in the heavy curtains. She had the distinct impression that something must have woken her and she rolled over on to her back and stared around the room. It seemed deserted, and realizing she was holding her breath she expelled it on a low sigh.

Then there was a terrific bang and she almost jumped out of her skin, jack-knifing upright in the bed, holding the covers closely to her chin. In heaven's name, what was that?

The sound seemed to have come from along the gallery and holding her lower lip between her teeth she climbed out of bed and groped blindly for her robe. Then she padded to the door and opened it nervously, prepared to slam it shut again if some unearthly being was waiting outside. But that was ridiculous, she told herself impatiently. No unearthly being would find a closed door any obstacle.

As she emerged on to the gallery, the bang came again and she sped along to the end where the spiral staircase was shrouded in shadow. And as a draught of cold air swept down on her she guessed, or thought she guessed, where the sound was coming from. Somehow the door to the battlements must have come open and the wind that moaned outside was causing it to bang against the wall and echo hollowly down the stone staircase.

She put a foot on the stairs to climb up and shut it when a thought occurred to her. She had secured the door firmly this afternoon. How could it have come open? Unless someone had opened it? But who?

Her heart almost stopped beating as the most ghastly thing of all occurred to her. She remembered how she had wondered whether anyone had ever thrown themselves from the battlements. She remembered Jonas's defeated expression, his silence at dinner; could he possibly have gone up there for such a purpose?

Her throat was dry and she could hardly swallow, but

she forced herself to climb the stairs. Then, as the open doorway seemed to confirm her worst fears, a dark figure appeared in the aperture outlined against the sky for a moment before he began to descend.

'Jonas?' she choked unsteadily. 'Jonas, are you all right?'

His head inclined in her direction. 'Julie?' His voice was cool. 'I'm sorry. Did the banging wake you? Someone hadn't secured the door properly and it came open. It leads to the battlements.'

As he turned to close the door, Julie nodded.

'Yes – yes, it – it was me. I went up there this afternoon. But – but I did lock it.'

Jonas came on down the stairs and she backed away from him until she reached the gallery. 'I expect the key got stuck,' he replied curtly. 'It sometimes does. And the force of the wind loosened the bolt. It's quite strong up there, but you'll be happy to hear that it's cleared the fog.'

Julie shivered. 'I – I – why were you on the battlements, Jonas? Why didn't you just close the door?'

Jonas's expression was impossible to read in the gloom. 'I was just checking to see that no one was up there, that's all. Why? What's it to you?'

Julie shook her head. She was near to tears. Reaction was setting in and she felt isolated and alone. The small hours had always had this devastating effect on her, she thought miserably, even though in the months after their separation she had become almost used to them. She had rarely slept before the pale light of dawn was lightening the horizon and this was going to be another of those nights, she felt sure of it.

He put out a hand suddenly, startling her, touching her arm where the wide sleeve of her gown was thrown back.

'You're frozen,' he exclaimed impatiently. 'And your feet are bare! These floors may be carpeted, but they're stone underneath and chilling. Do you want to catch your death of cold?'

Julie felt she didn't much care right then, but she said: 'I didn't stop to put on my mules.'

Jonas began to walk along the gallery and she had to move to keep up with him. 'Weren't you nervous?' he asked quietly.

Julie shrugged her shoulders. 'I – I was concerned.'

'About what?'

'I don't know. I had nightmares, I suppose. I didn't weigh up the possibilities, if that's what you mean.'

'Very commendable.' His tone was dry, and she wondered if he was mocking her. He halted by the door a few feet away from her own. 'This is my room. Good night.'

'Good night.' She brushed past him, hurrying to reach her door, but his voice stopped her.

'Is your fire still burning?'

Remembering the darkened room, Julie shook her head.

'Then come in here for a few minutes and get warm,' he offered abruptly.

Julie hesitated, but as he opened the door of his room and the light from within illuminated his withdrawn expression, she realized he expected her to refuse. And so she should, she thought, but instead she nodded and came back to where he was standing. A frown puckered his brow as he stood aside for her to enter his bedroom, but she ignored it and looked about her with real interest.

The room was smaller than the one she was occupying, but the bed was equally imposing. Obviously all the furniture in the bedrooms dated from the same period. The fire burned brightly in the grate and someone had just thrown on an armful of logs so that there was no likelihood of it dying for the next couple of hours. A book was lying on an armchair by the fire, and she guessed he had been reading when the door started banging. The knowledge was reassuring somehow. She had imagined he found no difficulty in sleeping.

She turned to take a surreptitious look at him. He was wearing the same woollen dressing gown he had worn the morning he had entered her bedroom, but although his feet and legs were bare he was wearing green leather slippers.

'Sit down,' he said, closing the door and indicating the chair where his book was lying. 'Just move the book. I can easily find the page I was reading later.'

Julie found a taper on the hearth and slipped it into the book as a marker. Then she put the book aside and perched on the edge of the chair. Jonas seated himself on the side of the bed some short distance away from her, but she could feel the probing intensity of his eyes upon her. He was probably wondering why she had accepted his invitation, she thought rather hysterically, but she didn't even know the answer to that herself. They sat in silence for five of the longest minutes Julie could ever remember experiencing and then he said: 'Well? Do you feel warmer now?'

Julie nodded. 'Very much, thank you.' She rose to her feet. 'I'd better be going. It's getting very late.'

'Yes.' Jonas made no attempt to detain her, but he stood up and his nearness caused a ripple of awareness to slide along her spine. It was such an intimate situation, she thought wildly. No one would believe that she and Jonas could be in such a situation without the inevitable happening.

'I – thank you again,' she stammered, moving awkwardly towards the door.

'It was nothing.' He was so cool, so unapproachable, so detached.

'Jonas—' she began nervously.

'Yes?'

'Couldn't – couldn't we part as – as friends?'

'You think I'm a liar. That's hardly a basis for friendship,' he replied grimly. 'But if you came in here for something else, then I'm willing to oblige.'

'Wh-what are you talking about?'

'You know well enough, Julie,' he retorted harshly. 'What are you? A frustrated neurotic – or can't you resist the temptation to experiment once more before it's too late?'

Julie gasped. 'Such a thought was never further from my mind! Just because – just because—'

'Just because you came into my bedroom in the middle of the night wearing only the minimum amount of covering, I shouldn't get the wrong ideas, is that it?' he taunted. 'What did you really want, Julie?'

'I wanted to get warm. And I had thought we – we might behave like civilized human beings,' she declared coldly. 'But I was wrong.'

Jonas shook his head. 'Oh, Julie, can't you do better than that?'

She took a deep breath. 'It's the truth. I – I know couples who – who are divorced who still meet regularly.'

'Do you? And that's what you mean by being civilized?'

'Yes—'

'Well, you chose the wrong man, Julie. I'm not like that.'

'Obviously not.' Julie reached for the handle, but he

interposed himself between her and the door, successfully preventing her from opening it. A twinge of apprehension pricked her, but she ignored it and said rather tremulously: 'Please get out of my way.'

'And if I choose not to?' He put out a hand and she flinched as he fingered the silky texture of the hair that fell softly over her shoulder.

'Jonas – please—' She felt driven beyond bearing.

'Please? Please what?'

His hands curved behind her nape drawing her towards him. The pressure on her neck was more brutal than loving and when she tried to move her head she stifled a gasp of agony as pain shot simultaneously into her head and down to her shoulders. She lost her balance and fell against him, immediately feeling the hardening of his thighs through the materials that separated them. His hands became gentler, moving caressingly over her shoulders to her back, to her hips, holding her closer, her face against the parting lapels of his dressing gown.

'Dear God, Julie,' he groaned, and with one hand he gripped her throat, turning her face up to his. His mouth came down on hers and although she knew she ought not to respond she couldn't help herself. Her lips parted and he kissed her hungrily, awakening urges inside her which had lain dormant for a long time. Her hands encountered the cord of his gown and her fingers closed round it. 'Unfasten it,' he said against her ear, and her blood was like a thunder in her ears.

'I – I – *no*!'

With a supreme effort she wrenched herself free of him and while he was still staring at her in a dazed way she dragged open the door and fled from the room. Her room had a key and she turned it, but she knew deep inside her that it wouldn't be necessary.

CHAPTER SEVEN

JULIE went to bed, but she scarcely slept and was up just after seven taking a bath. Her blouse and suit had still not been returned to her, so she was forced to examine the contents of the wardrobe again. She took out a dark red jersey slack suit and a navy silk blouse to wear with it. Then she coiled her hair into a chignon, and forcing herself to remain calm unlocked her bedroom door, walked along the gallery and down the stairs.

To her surprise a tan calf suitcase was standing in the hall. It didn't belong to her and her brows drew together perplexedly. Had Jonas got an unexpected visitor?

Her nerves tightening, she opened the living-room door. There was no one about and biting her lip she walked along the hall to the dining-room. It was empty, too, and she continued on her way to the kitchen. The Macphersons were bound to be up and know what was going on.

She heard voices as she reached the Macphersons' living-room and she passed through it tentatively and put her head round the kitchen door. Jonas was seated opposite Rob Macpherson at the kitchen table tackling a plate of kidneys and bacon. The bandage had disappeared from his hand and in its place was a wide stretch of Elastoplast. Mrs. Macpherson was busy frying bacon at the stove, but she caught a glimpse of Julie out of the corner of her eye and said:

'Well, Mrs. Hunter, you're an early riser!' She glanced towards Jonas. 'Couldn't either of you sleep?'

Julie's eyes flickered nervously over Jonas, too, but

after a brief hard look at her he resumed eating. 'I – er – as I'm leaving today, I thought I'd – make an early start,' she stumbled.

'Yes, I know.' Mrs. Macpherson's mouth turned down at the corners. 'Not that I approve, mind you.'

Julie sighed. Jonas had told them. But what had he said?

'I have my work to do, Mrs. Macpherson,' she managed awkwardly.

'I realize that.' Mrs. Macpherson clicked her tongue. 'But Mr. Hunter's not fit to be driving all that way. His hand's not half healed—'

'*Driving!*' Julie was totally confused. 'I don't—'

'I'm driving you to London, Julie.' Jonas's eyes held hers now, defying her to argue with him. 'I can't let you go all that way alone, not after you made the journey here.'

Julie gasped. 'I don't mind—'

'But I do.' Jonas's face was grim. 'Would you have these people think me completely selfish?'

Julie made a helpless gesture. Without creating an open confrontation with him here, in front of the Macphersons, there was little she could say. And what was his motive anyway? After last night she had expected nothing more from him.

'Well, come along in and sit down,' exclaimed Mrs. Macpherson, spearing bacon on to a plate. 'Don't just hover there in the doorway. I expect a nice cup of tea wouldn't come amiss. It's a cold morning. But at least it's clear.'

Rob Macpherson patted the chair beside him. 'Come and sit here, Mrs. Hunter. Tell me what you think of Castle Lochcraig.'

Julie was glad to get off legs which had grown decidedly shaky. 'I – er – it's beautiful,' she murmured abstractedly.

'Ay, it is.' Rob lay back in his chair with some satisfaction. 'I never grow tired of the view across the loch early in the morning. With the sun rising over Ben Drossan. Och! It's a bonny sight.'

Julie linked her hands together in her lap and looked down at them. Jonas was finishing his meal, thickly buttering a slice of toast, adding some homemade marmalade, drinking a mug of steaming tea. He scarcely seemed aware of her presence and she wished she had the nerve to say that she had no intention of driving all the way to London with him – that she was going to take the train to Inverness as she had planned to do.

Mrs. Macpherson provided her with a cup of tea and said: 'And what will it be, Mrs. Hunter? Scrambled eggs, bacon, kidneys?'

'Oh – nothing to eat, thank you.'

'You have to eat something,' protested the housekeeper.

Jonas looked up. 'Bring my wife some toast, Mrs. Macpherson,' he directed coolly.

Julie glared at him as the housekeeper turned away to do as he asked. 'I'm not hungry,' she insisted.

'You can't begin a five-hundred-mile journey on an empty stomach,' he retorted curtly. 'As I recall, you're not always the best of travellers.'

Julie pursed her lips. Trust Jonas to remember that awful occasion when she had developed car sickness on a trip to his mother's home in Yorkshire. She had gone down with 'flu a couple of days later and afterwards she had put the sickness down to that. But now Jonas was speaking as though it was a common occurrence, and it simply wasn't. In consequence, when Mrs. Macpherson brought the toast Julie ignored it, and no amount of silent adjuration from Jonas could make her do otherwise. Instead she drank three cups of strong tea and accepted one of Rob's cigarettes. She didn't like it. It made her cough. But at least it gave her something to do with her hands.

Afterwards Jonas accompanied her out into the hall, advising the housekeeper over his shoulder that they would be leaving in half an hour.

'That was rather childish, wasn't it?' he queried dryly, as they walked towards the tower hallway.

'I've told you, I'm not hungry,' she retorted. 'And I wish you wouldn't make arrangements without first consulting me.'

'Would you have agreed?'

'You know I wouldn't.'

'Enough said.' Jonas's tone was sardonic and he nodded to where his suitcase was standing. 'Have you finished packing?'

'I still haven't had my clothes returned to me.'

Jonas's lips twisted. 'That ghastly suit! You don't want that, do you? The clothes you're wearing belong to you, as I'm sure you're aware.'

Julie's resolve weakened and then she mentally stiffened her shoulders. 'The suit is the one I wear for business.'

'Business?' His lips twitched. 'How formal! Thank God I'm out of that rat-race. All right, I'll give you back the suit, and the shirt that goes with it, providing you promise not to wear them to travel in.'

'I don't have to make any bargains with you!' she exclaimed hotly.

'Don't you?'

Julie flushed and compressed her lips. 'Oh – oh, very well. Where are they?'

'In my bedroom. Do you want to get them?'

Julie turned away. 'No. No, you get them. I'll wait in the living-room.'

'All right.'

He moved his shoulders indifferently and she went into the living-room feeling unaccountably chastened.

Rob accompanied them across to the mainland so that he could fetch the outboard motor boat back to the island for his own use. He waited until Jonas had reversed the powerful sports car out of the garage and then closed the doors and came to shake hands with both of them.

'Come back soon, Mrs. Hunter,' he said warmly. 'It's been nice having another woman about the place again.'

'Thank you.' Julie glanced awkwardly at Jonas as she got into the car. 'I – er – you've been very kind.'

Jonas put the car into gear and as they drove away Rob raised his hand. Unaccountably, Julie felt a lump come into her throat. The Macphersons were such nice people, such *honest* people; she hated deceiving them like this.

They drove for some distance before Julie could bring herself to say: 'Would you like me to take over for a while later on? To give your hand a rest?'

Jonas shook his head. 'That won't be necessary. There's no pain.'

Judging by the lines beside his mouth, Julie was sure there must be, but she could hardly argue with him about something like that. She glanced sideways at him. Travelling along like this it was all too easy to remember other occasions when they had driven together. Once Jonas had had an assignment in Vienna and they had taken the car to the continent and driven south through Belgium and Germany to Austria, staying at small hotels and *pensions*, almost making a second honeymoon of the trip. Her nerves jarred. They had been so happy. How could he have destroyed that happiness for the sake of one night?

She stared blindly out of the car windows. Like Mrs. Macpherson had said it was a clear morning. The mountains looked stark and rugged, paling towards the peaks where the watery sun glinted on layers of snow. Only the pine trees were deeply green, standing like sentinels beside the wide stretches of brackish water.

They stopped for lunch soon after twelve. Julie was relieved, although she said nothing. For the past hour she had been feeling distinctly queasy, and the taste of the strong tea Mrs. Macpherson had provided was still in the back of her throat. They stopped at a hotel just outside of Fort William and Julie, reflecting how much further they still had to go, had to force down a feeling of panic.

The meal they were offered was plain but good, although all Julie could manage was some vegetable soup and a little of the steak. She refused a dessert and watching Jonas eat a chocolate pudding made her feel quite sick. Throughout the meal, Jonas consulted a road map on the table beside him, obviously intent on finding the quickest route, and Julie was left to her own devices. Then it was out to the car again and on to the next leg of their journey.

They crossed the ferry at Ballachulish and turned inland, leaving the sea lochs behind. They drove down through Tyndrum and Crianlarich, through beautiful mountainous country that Julie was scarcely aware of, and reached the shores of Loch Lomond. The road that ran beside the loch twisted and turned and Julie could feel the sickness she had thought she was managing to control rising in her throat again.

'Oh, Jonas,' she moaned desperately, 'could you stop the car for a minute?'

Jonas stood on his brakes, bringing the car to a halt on a grassy verge between pine trees. Julie didn't wait to explain. She unfastened her seat belt, thrust open the door and stumbled out. She was hardly aware that Jonas had come to stand beside her until he said: 'How do you feel now?'

She wiped her mouth with a tissue and dabbed at her watering eyes. 'I'm – I'm all right. You don't have to tell me. I know I should have had some breakfast.'

'Get in the car,' he said roughly. 'I'm not completely without sensibilities, you know.'

Julie got back in reluctantly, but at least the sickly feeling had receded even if it hadn't left her altogether. Jonas leant across and fastened her harness and then looked into her eyes intently.

'What kind of a brute do you think I am?' he demanded.

Julie felt near to tears. 'I – I don't think you're a – a brute at all.'

Jonas studied her a moment longer and then he swung round in his seat and fastened his own safety belt. 'Okay,' he said. 'We'll take it a little less recklessly, right?'

Julie nodded and settled back, ridiculously warmed by his evident concern.

Exhaustion both from the sickness and her sleepless night eventually took its toll of her and she fell asleep. When she opened her eyes again, her neck was stiff and it was dark outside the car. Only their headlamps, and the headlamps of cars they were passing, illuminated the road.

Blinking, she sat up and said: 'Where are we?'

Jonas glanced sideways at her. 'We're on the A66. Approaching Scotch Corner.'

'Scotch Corner?' Julie stared stupidly at the clock on the dash. 'But that's in north Yorkshire, isn't it? I didn't know we went anywhere near there. I thought we came down through Carlisle and Kendal.'

'We would – if we were heading straight for London,' he agreed briefly.

'But where are we going?' Julie was too shocked to register the time at that moment.

'To Howard's Green. It's only about another fifteen miles.'

'Howard's – Green!' Julie licked her lips. 'But – but that's your mother's home.'

'I am aware of that.' He was dry.

Julie stared at his profile. 'I can't go there!'

'Why not?'

'You know why not. Jonas, I can't. You know how upset she was when – when we split up.'

'I know. But she's got used to the idea now.'

'Even so—' Julie stared through the darkened windows. Then she turned her attention to the clock again. 'It's almost half past seven. We can't simply impose ourselves on your mother!'

'Why not? You forget, it's my home.'

Julie shook her head. 'But why are we going there?'

'Would you believe – I'm tired?'

'Oh, *Jonas*!' Concerned with her own selfish anxieties, she had forgotten all about his hand. She sighed. 'Couldn't I take over?'

'No. I know this road. I can make it.'

His voice sounded strained and she again found herself in a defensive position. All the same, they could have stayed at a hotel. It would certainly have been easier for her. But to voice such a suggestion now was impossible.

Particularly when she considered how far he had driven while she slept.

They left the main road a couple of miles further on and followed a quieter, winding road through several villages before reaching Howard's Burn. The Hunter house, Howard's Green, stood on the outskirts of the village, a rambling grey stone building set among trees with perhaps an acre of land attached to it where Mrs. Hunter grew roses and kept a few chickens. Tall elms shielded the front of the house from the road and as Jonas turned between the stone gateposts Julie saw that the gates stood wide as usual. There were lights in the downstairs windows and as the curtains were seldom drawn she saw Jonas's mother come to peer out as the headlights swept the forecourt and Jonas brought the powerful vehicle to a halt at the foot of the steps leading up to the front door.

Then he slumped, resting his forehead on the steering wheel, his shoulders hunched in an attitude of exhaustion. Julie turned to him anxiously, but before she could touch him or ask him what was wrong light streamed down on them and Mrs. Hunter came down the steps from the open door. She pulled open Jonas's door and was saying: 'Jonas, what a surprise—' when she saw him slumped across the wheel. 'Oh, my God! Jonas, what's happened?'

Jonas raised his head and now Julie could see the grim lines of fatigue beside his mouth and eyes. 'I'm all right, Mother,' he averred, thrusting his legs out of the car and getting out to give her a hug. 'Tired, that's all. It's good to see you. How are you?'

Mrs. Hunter looked up at him rather worriedly and then shook her head. 'Are you sure you're all right, Jonas?' Then at his impatient nod, she added: 'I'm fine –

fine.' She squeezed his forearms. 'Oh, it is good to see you, Jonas. It's been almost three months.'

She was a small woman, thin and wiry, her greying brown hair secured in a knot on top of her head. She had been quite a beauty in her youth, but life in terms of her estrangement from her family and more recently her husband's death had etched a tracery of lines across her face. But she was still a handsome woman for her age and her slender figure enabled her to look elegant in the most casual of clothes. But none of her sons had taken after her. They were all tall like Professor Hunter had been, and as Jonas was the eldest and her firstborn, he was the one she truly favoured even though she would have been the last to admit it.

Now her grey eyes flickered towards the car and Julie could feel herself shrinking. She had realized that Mrs. Hunter had noticed someone else in the car with Jonas, but as yet she did not know her identity.

Jonas, impatient to get introductions over with, said: 'Come on out, Julie. Mother, Julie's with me. We'd like to stay overnight if you've no objections.'

Mrs. Hunter's face mirrored her amazement as Julie got reluctantly out the car and came round to the others. 'Julie!' she exclaimed, and then looked incredulously at her son. 'You don't mean—'

'I don't mean anything,' said Jonas heavily, walking to the boot of the car and unlocking it and taking out their suitcases. 'Could we go inside? It's cold out here.'

He went ahead up the steps, but Mrs. Hunter continued to stare at her daughter-in-law. 'Julie,' she said again, shaking her head. 'This really is a surprise.'

Julie tortured the strap of her handbag, not knowing whether to shake hands with her mother-in-law or kiss her or what. 'I – I'm sorry about this, Mrs. Hunter,' she began awkwardly. 'But we've been driving since early this morning – down from Scotland – and Jonas was exhausted – he cut his hand a couple of days ago, you see—'

'Jonas cut his hand? Nothing serious, I hope.'

'I – I don't think so. It was on a – on a glass. He's got two stitches in his palm – and he was so tired – and he said you probably wouldn't mind—'

She was stumbling on, hot and embarrassed, unable to think of any good reason why they should be here. But Mrs. Hunter merely patted her hand and began to climb the steps and Julie had to accompany her.

'Bless you, child, I don't mind,' she said reassuringly. 'I'm always glad of the company. Since the boys got married or moved away, this house often seems empty. But I don't understand. You've been up in Scotland, you say? Staying with Jonas?'

Julie's cheeks burned. 'In – in a manner of speaking, yes.'

Mrs. Hunter shrugged, obviously perplexed, but they had reached the entrance hall and as she closed the door behind them Jonas came out of the room to their left. The cases were standing at the foot of the stairs and rather than look at them Julie looked rather desperately round the attractive hallway. Cream paper looked good against dark wood, and the apple green carpet spread into every corner and up the stairs.

Apparently deciding that explanations could wait until later, Mrs. Hunter moved towards him saying: 'Have you had anything to eat? You look positively worn out!'

'No.' Jonas shook his head. He had shed his black leather driving coat and in the navy suede suit and cream shirt he looked pale and heavy-eyed, but no less attractive, thought Julie bitterly. 'Er – Julie was sick earlier. I don't think she should have anything heavy.'

'I'm all right.' Julie had to say something. She unfastened the jacket of her suit. 'Do you think I could have a wash? I feel filthy.'

'Of course, of course.' Mrs. Hunter switched on the upstairs lights. 'You know where the bathroom is. I'll come up in a minute and make up the bed – beds.' She pressed her lips together. 'You can come into the kitchen with me, Jonas, and tell me what you've been doing.'

Guessing that Jonas would explain the situation to his mother, Julie went thankfully up the stairs. The bathroom was large and old-fashioned, but the plumbing was not. There was plenty of hot water and warm towels and it was marvellous to wash away the grime of the journey and comb out her hair. The sleep she had had, had refreshed her, and she found the thought of food was not as distasteful as it had been several hours ago. It was strange being in this house again, though. She and Jonas had stayed here lots of times before. She had always got along well with his mother, and his father too, when he was alive. His brothers, three of them, and all younger than Jonas, had usually been away at college, and later two of them had married and the third had become an archaeologist and spent most of his time on some dig or other. Mrs. Hunter had coped very well after her husband died. She was an independent sort of person, not given to self-pity, and she had always looked after this house herself except for having a woman come in a couple of times a week to tackle the rough work.

Julie secured her hair in the chignon again, checked that her suit did not have too many creases after the long journey, and then went back downstairs. There was the unmistakable smell of meat and vegetables in the hall and she hesitated uncertainly. In the old days she would have bounced into the kitchen and demanded to know what it was, but things were different now. Instead, she went into the lounge and seated herself in a comfortable chintz-covered armchair by the fire. Although there was a very adequate heating system installed, Mrs. Hunter had always insisted on keeping one coal fire and this one was burning merrily. Mrs. Hunter's knitting was lying untidily on the settee, and magazines spilled out of the rack beside the hearth. Firelight winked on the polished wood of a baby grand piano in one corner, while the walls were panelled and covered with prints. Long faded velvet curtains edged the tall windows, falling to the now worn beauty of an Indian carpet. It was a comfortable, lived-in sort of room, and Julie had always thought that when she had children of her own and brought them here to see their grandmother she would not have to worry too much if sticky fingers explored in forbidden places. Her fingers curled. Well, there was no likelihood of that now. But the remembrance of those girlish thoughts could still arouse pain . . . and it shouldn't.

She was staring into the flames when Jonas came into the room. He had shed his jacket now and taken off his tie, the unfastened neck of his shirt revealing the slender silver chain that supported the medallion.

Julie looked up nervously. 'I – er – how do you feel?'

Jonas shrugged, flexing his shoulder muscles. 'I'm tired, that's all. Nothing to worry about. I'll take a bath later. That should relax me.'

'What about your hand?'

Jonas exhibited the elastic plaster. 'It feels stiff, that's all. Natural enough in the circumstances.'

Julie nodded and bent her head. 'Have – have you – er – told your mother—?'

'About us? Of course.' Jonas went to help himself to a drink from a tray of bottles and glasses on a nearby table.

'Do you want something? Sherry, perhaps?'

'No, thanks.' Julie sighed. 'What did she say?'

Jonas poured himself some Scotch. 'Nothing much. What did you expect her to say?'

'She doesn't – well, object to me being here?'

Jonas turned, raising the glass to his lips. 'Could you imagine it?'

'No, but you are her son, and I – well, you know what I mean.'

'I think so. Nevertheless, my mother is not like yours.' He swallowed most of his Scotch at a gulp.

'What's that supposed to mean?'

'Could you imagine your mother welcoming me back into the fold?'

'No – but that's different.'

'How is it? Because you were the innocent party? Well, I'm sorry to disappoint you, but *my* mother believes me. So far as she's concerned, you were wrong.'

Julie hunched her shoulders. 'Oh, well, I don't suppose it matters.'

'No.' Jonas turned back to pour another drink. 'No, nothing matters any more, does it?'

Julie had no time to reply to this cryptic statement before Mrs. Hunter appeared in the doorway. 'It's ready,' she announced with a smile. 'I thought we could eat in the kitchen, if you don't mind. It's warmer in there. I've not been using the dining-room much myself.'

They sat in the kitchen, round the square scrubbed table where Julie had often watched her mother-in-law making bread. There was new bread this evening, and bowls of thick beefy broth, and breakfast cups of coffee. Julie found she was hungry, in spite of everything, and she enjoyed the simple meal better than she would some formal dinner at a hotel. She supposed she ought to feel grateful to Jonas for bringing her here. After all, he must have guessed that after being sick she would not want too many eyes upon her, but as usual she had argued with him over it.

During the meal, Mrs. Hunter relieved the tension by asking Jonas about his new book and when the first one was going to begin filming. They were questions Julie had asked, but she found his replies as interesting as ever. Or perhaps it was that he had such an attractive speaking voice that anything he said was interesting to her ears.

When the meal was over, Julie offered to wash up, but Mrs. Hunter wouldn't hear of it. 'I can manage these few things,' she insisted. 'Come along. I'll show you where you're going to sleep. Then when you're ready you can go to bed.'

The room Julie was given had been Paul's, the youngest son. There were still pictures of revolutionary heroes on the walls and a collection of photographs of sporting teams from college days. Mrs. Hunter left her to open her suitcase and take out her night things and Julie guessed she was hoping she would go to bed soon so that she might have some time alone with her son. Deciding that this was the least she could do in the circumstances, Julie went downstairs again only long enough to say good night and saw the look of relief on Mrs. Hunter's face. Jonas's expression was less easy to read, but he inclined his head politely and she went back upstairs again feeling cut off from them and unloved.

Because she had slept that afternoon in the car she was not particularly tired, so she examined the contents of the bookcase. As well as Paul's books there was a book of Rupert Brooke's poems which belonged to her mother-in-law and the words on the flyleaf brought a lump to her throat. It read: *To my favourite confidante from your son, Jonas.*

She found it hard to read after that and putting the book aside lay back on her pillows. Neither Jonas nor his mother had come to bed yet and knowing how tired Jonas was she hoped his mother would not keep him up much longer. About half an hour later she was relieved to hear someone mounting the stairs, and she heard water running in the bathroom. She remembered that Jonas had said he was going to have a bath before going to bed and she wriggled lower under the covers.

She heard Mrs. Hunter come up some time later and go to her room, and then later still she heard Jonas enter his bedroom. For a moment when he had crossed the landing from the bathroom she had wondered whether he might see her light and come to her door, but he didn't. She drew a tremulous breath. What was the matter with her?

She almost jumped out of her skin a few minutes later when her bedroom door did open and Jonas stood there. Dressed only in a towelling bathrobe, he looked big and disturbingly handsome, and her toes curled beneath the covers. Then she saw he was holding a roll of adhesive plaster in his hand.

'Y—yes?' she managed.

Jonas looked down at the plaster. 'I have to change the dressing,' he said quietly. 'Could you help me with it? I saw your light or I shouldn't have bothered you.'

'I – it's no bother.' Julie sat up in bed jerkily. 'You – you'd better close the door. We don't want to disturb your mother.'

'No.' His tone was dry, but he did as she asked and came over to the bed. 'I've taken the wet one off. If you could just bind this piece right round my palm and the back of my hand.'

Julie took his hand in hers. He had the hands of an artist, lean and long-fingered, and tanned, too, after his months in South America. Trying to ignore the way touching him made her pulses race, she turned his hand over and gasped at the ugly inflammation in his palm.

'It looks worse than it is,' he said patiently, sitting down on the side of the bed. 'Gripping the wheel all day hasn't helped.'

Julie looked up at him, but his face was too close, his eyes too penetrating, and she quickly looked down again. 'Do – don't you put anything on it? Ointment – something like that?'

'No. You know the doctor gave me some antibiotics. They're all I need. Just put on the plaster, will you?'

He was so cool, while she was a burning mass of nerves and sensations. Her tongue protruded slightly as she concentrated on securing the plaster firmly without hurting him too much. Then she let go of his hand and rubbed her own moist palms together. 'There you are!'

'Thanks.' He rose to his feet.

'Jonas—' Now why had she said his name?

'Yes?' He looked down at her.

'Oh, nothing.' She moved her shoulders in a dismissing motion. 'I hope it's all right.'

'It will be.' He walked to the door. 'Good night, Julie.'

'Good night.'

The door closed behind him and Julie found she was trembling. This was ridiculous, she thought irritably. She was becoming neurotic, just like he said. Then a thought struck her. At the bottom of her handbag there was a bottle containing sleeping pills. If she took a couple of them she would be sure of getting some sleep. But her handbag was downstairs . . .

She thrust her legs out of bed. There was no point in lying there, waiting for the pills to come to her. And equally, she could not bear the thought of lying awake again. Pushing her feet into her mules, she opened the bedroom door and went silently across the landing and down the stairs. Her handbag was lying on the chair in the lounge where she had left it, and as the firelight illuminated the room she didn't need to put on the light. She fumbled in the bottom of her bag, impatient when the tiny bottle kept slipping out of her reach. But at last she got hold of it and brought it out, unscrewing the cap. The pills were small and white, lethal-looking little tablets containing a measured dose of some narcotic. It crossed her mind with the inconsequence of such things that a careless overdose would solve all her problems ...

'What are you doing?'

Jonas's harsh tones almost petrified her. He stood in the doorway, still wearing the towelling robe, his hand resting on the switch which had suddenly dissipated the shadows and cast a brilliant illumination over the room.

Julie swallowed convulsively. 'I – I – my handbag was down here,' she stammered.

'Why should you need your handbag at this time of night?' His eyes narrowed as they took in the small bottle in her fingers. 'What are you taking?'

Julie sighed. 'Just – just a headache tablet,' she lied uncomfortably.

He walked towards her. 'Let me see.'

'No.' She thrust the bottle back into the bag and concealed the hand containing the two tablets she had extracted behind her back.

Jonas ignored her, taking the bag forcibly from her and

flinging it on to the settee. Then he twisted her arm from behind her back and opened her clenched fingers. 'Those are not headache tablets,' he stated grimly, looking down at what lay on her palm. 'They're sedatives, aren't they?'

She held up her head. 'What if they are?'

'You shouldn't be taking sedatives, Julie,' he muttered roughly. He walked across and threw the two tablets into the fire. 'Now, go on – get back to bed!'

Julie rubbed her wrist where his grip had reddened the flesh. 'I'm not a child, you know, Jonas,' she declared indignantly.

Then she saw her handbag lying on the couch. Without stopping to consider her actions, she snatched up the bag and was half-way up the stairs when she heard him coming after her. She fled into her bedroom and closed the door, searching desperately for a key. But there wasn't one, and she was standing tremblingly in the middle of the floor when the door opened. Jonas came into the room, closing the door behind him and leaning back against it for an unbearable moment of truth.

Then he straightened and came towards her, jerking the bag out of her hands. 'I'm not stupid, you know,' he snapped. 'I am aware that you've got some more.'

Julie watched as he extracted the small bottle and slipped it into the pocket of his robe. Then her control snapped. 'Oh – oh, please, Jonas,' she begged, 'don't take them all. I – I couldn't bear another night like – like last night!'

Jonas stared at her disbelievingly, his dark brows drawing together above the narrowed glitter of his eyes. Then he reached for her, dragging her closely against him, pressing his hot face into her neck. They stood like that for a long minute and Julie could feel her traitorous body yielding to the hardness of his. Then his mouth moved up her throat and found hers, parting her lips and devouring them.

After that, Julie didn't much care what he did to her so long as she could be close to him like this. She pressed herself against him, aware of the fine thread of control he was exercising, aware of her power to arouse him almost against his will.

'For God's sake, Julie,' he muttered, 'do you want me to stay?'

Julie wound her bare arms around his neck, inviting his possession. 'Oh, yes,' she groaned feverishly. 'Stay with me, Jonas, make love to me . . .'

His control snapped and with an exclamation almost of protest, he lifted her on to the bed and slid on to it beside her. 'Julie . . .' he began, huskily, but she silenced his mouth with her fingers.

'Love me, Jonas,' she breathed, unloosening his robe. 'Love me – do it, Jonas, now . . .'

CHAPTER EIGHT

WHEN Julie opened her eyes next morning, brilliant autumn sunlight was flooding into the bedroom. A delicious feeling of lassitude was upon her and as full recollection of the events of the night before returned, she turned her head swiftly to where Jonas's head had rested on the pillow beside hers. But Jonas was gone, and because it was a single bed there was nothing to show that he had spent the night with her.

A terrible sense of desolation assailed her. Where was he? She couldn't possibly have imagined it all, could she? But no – as she moved her limbs still tingled from the pressure of his hands, the weight of his powerful body; and her lips were bruised from the passionate hunger of his mouth. Oh yes, she thought languorously, recalling every moment of that urgent possession. It had been real, satisfyingly so . . . but what now?

She pushed the question aside. She didn't want to think of that now. She wanted to take everything as it came. She didn't know what she had committed herself to, whether her surrender was an acceptance that her need for him was stronger than her revulsion against his guilt. She only knew that she still loved him as much as ever, and that no other man would ever be able to arouse her as he could arouse her.

She rolled on to her stomach taking the covers with her, and stared incredulously at the clock on the bedside table. It couldn't possibly be a quarter to eleven, could it? She sat backwards on her heels with a jolt and then crossed her arms protectively across her breasts as the cool air hit her naked body.

With a disturbing sense of apprehension she slid out of bed and pulled on her dressing gown. Why had no one woken her? She ought to have been up by this time. She padded to the door and pulled it open, standing silent for a few moments, listening. But the only sound coming from downstairs was that of a radio.

Unable to stand the suspense of waiting until she was dressed to find out where Jonas was, Julie left her room and went down the stairs, peering hopefully into the lounge. There was no one about and deciding that the radio was playing in the kitchen she made her way there. She opened the kitchen door and found Mrs. Hunter peeling potatoes at the sink, but of Jonas there was no sign.

Hearing the door open, her mother-in-law looked round. 'Oh, so you're awake at last, Julie. I was just going to finish these and then bring you up a nice cup of tea.'

Julie looked down apologetically at her dressing gown. 'I – er – I overslept. I didn't even stop to get dressed . . .'

'That doesn't matter. Come along in. It's nice and warm in here. And there's just the two of us. Mrs. Carter doesn't come in today as it's Saturday, and Jonas had to leave for London over an hour ago.'

Julie's lips parted. 'Jonas – has gone?'

'That's right.' Mrs. Hunter turned down the radio and lifting the kettle began to fill it from the tap. 'He spoke to his agent on the phone this morning and there's some problem he needs help with. He apologized for having to leave you behind, but it was rather urgent and he didn't want to disturb you. He said you hadn't been sleeping too well.'

Julie plumped down into a chair, her legs giving out on her. 'But – but I was going to London, too,' she protested dazedly, scarcely able to think of anything at that moment but that he had left her.

'I know, dear,' said Mrs. Hunter comfortably, 'but there are plenty of trains, and I can easily drive you to Darlington station when you're ready to leave. You don't have any deadline to keep, do you?'

Julie shook her head slowly. Suddenly the events of the night before were not something to contemplate with anything but self-disgust. She almost cringed when she recalled how wantonly she had behaved, betraying herself, and those nearest and dearest to her. How could she have forgotten the things she had drilled into herself on her journey north, the warnings she had been given, the fear that something like this might happen? And now he had achieved his objective, he had left her, just as she had known he would ...

'What's the matter, Julie? You're looking very pale.'

Mrs. Hunter was staring at her with evident concern and Julie forced herself to shake her head, bringing a little blood back to her drained cheeks. 'It's nothing,' she denied, smoothing the table top with her finger tips. 'I – how have you been keeping? Do you see much of Nicholas and Joanne these days?'

Mrs. Hunter was clearly not satisfied with Julie's attempt to change the topic of conversation, but she said she saw her second son and his wife at least once every week, and that their baby girl, Penny, was cutting her first teeth. Then she returned to the attack.

'Julie, I want you to tell me something – truthfully – are you still in love with Jonas? I'm an interfering old woman, I know, but I couldn't help but notice how the news of his leaving affected you—'

Julie wouldn't look at her. 'I – I was surprised, that's all.'

'Was that all?' Mrs. Hunter's eyes were almost as penetrating as her son's. Julie could feel them boring into her.

'I really don't think you should ask me that,' she murmured uncomfortably.

'Why not? He's my son, Julie, I love him dearly. I know you've hurt him, badly, and I want to know why. If you're still in love with him—'

'I – I don't know that I am—'

'Don't you?' Mrs. Hunter turned away to make the tea. 'All right, we'll say no more about it.'

Julie sighed. 'Mrs. Hunter, I didn't break up our marriage—'

'No. Angela Forrest did that.'

Julie gasped. 'How can you say such a thing? You can't blame Angela for – for something Jonas did!'

Mrs. Hunter stirred the teapot vigorously. 'What did he do?'

Julie bent her head. 'You know as well as I do—'

'You're very willing to condemn my son, aren't you, Julie?'

Julie flushed. 'You know how Jonas attracts women!'

'Oh, yes. Women are attracted to him, I'll give you that. But how many women has he been attracted to?'

'How should I know?' Julie shook her head. 'Lots, I suppose.'

Mrs. Hunter poured her a cup of tea and pushed it briskly towards her, so briskly that some of it slopped into the saucer. 'You lived with Jonas for two years, Julie. Didn't you learn anything about him in that time? How many times did you find him making love to other women, coming home late, telling you lies?'

Julie raised her cup to her lips. 'Only once.'

'The night he spent with Angela Forrest?'

'Yes.'

'Have you never stopped to consider that she might be lying?'

'Of course.'

'But you dismissed the idea?'

'Yes.'

'Why?'

Julie put down her cup. 'Angela and I have been friends since we were children, Mrs. Hunter. Jonas is asking me to believe that she deliberately waited until I was out of town for the night before coming to the apartment, feigning collapse, and allowing him to look after her. I ask you, does it sound reasonable?'

Mrs. Hunter seated herself opposite. 'It sounds damning,' she admitted, nodding. 'But we have an old-fashioned notion in this country that a man should be considered innocent until he's proved guilty.'

'Don't you think his guilt is proved?'

'No. Words can mean anything. As I see it, it's a simple case of Angela's word against his.'

'Not entirely.'

'What do you mean?'

'I mean – there was something more.' Julie felt sick even thinking about it after last night. 'I – I got a letter.'

'A letter?' Mrs. Hunter stared at her uncomprehendingly.

'Yes. A letter. One of those ghastly anonymous things. I – I tore it up.' She had told no one about that, not even her mother.

'What did it say?'

Julie looked down into her cup. 'Oh, you know the sort of thing,' she mumbled chokily. '*Do you know your husband is having an affair with your best friend?* It was horrible!'

'Did you ever find out who sent it?'

'No. How could I? I destroyed it. No one saw it but me.'

'When did it arrive?'

'That morning – the morning I came back and found – and found—'

'I see.' Mrs. Hunter digested this silently. 'I wonder who could have sent such a letter.'

'I don't know, and I don't really care.' Julie finished her tea and pushed her cup aside, getting to her feet. 'Could you possibly run me to the station this morning? I – I'd like to get the first train back to London. I expect Jonas told you I went to Scotland to get an interview for the magazine I work for. I've got to get it typed out and presentable to give Mark on Monday morning. Mark Bernstein, that is, my boss.'

Mrs. Hunter sighed heavily. 'I hoped you would stay the week-end, Julie. No matter what happens between you and Jonas, I'm very fond of you, you know.'

Julie shook her head jerkily. 'You're very kind, but I really do have to get back.'

'All right.' Mrs. Hunter didn't try to dissuade her although her lined face wore an expression of regret. 'But if ever you would like to come back – for a visit, perhaps – feel free to do so.'

Later in the day, sitting in the train on her way to London, Julie half wished she had accepted her mother-in-law's offer. It would have been quite a relief to spend a few days in such undemanding company. This past week in Scotland had not improved her nervous system, and the prospect of seeing her mother and Angela again after what had taken place between herself and Jonas filled her with apprehension. Would she be able to convince them that her stay at the castle had been unavoidable, and would she manage to hide the highly emotional state in which she now found herself?

She took a taxi from King's Cross to the Victorian mansion in Pallister Court where she had her flat. The traffic in London on this busy Saturday evening was as hectic as ever and Julie was glad when she could pay off the driver and climb the stairs to her first-floor apartment. And yet, for all that, she was almost reluctant to begin her normal life again. Was it really less than a week since she left here? It seemed much longer than that.

She inserted her key in the lock and entered the tiny entrance hall. 'Angela?' she called tentatively. 'Angela, are you there?'

But to her relief, there was no reply, and she realized the flat was empty. She entered the living-room and looked about her without enthusiasm. It was an attractive room, but after the spacious elegance of the rooms at the castle, it seemed small and badly lit. Outside, the roar of traffic drifted from the main thoroughfare a hundred yards away, while opposite the lights of a similar apartment building blocked her view.

Julie drew the curtains, impatient with herself for feeling so depressed. She could easily take a holiday if she wanted one, find some hotel with a magnificent view and take things easy for a couple of weeks. But that wasn't what she wanted, and the knowledge frightened her. She had always considered herself sane and sensible. She had maintained an aloof self-control all through the difficult weeks after her separation from Jonas, and now, after only a few days in his company, she was letting doubt enter her mind. Not doubt about his guilt, although that could trouble her too, if she let it; no – doubt as to whether their separation had been the only solution. Might she have been more understanding, more forgiving? Without the intervention of others, might she have accepted his lapse for what it was because she needed him more than her pride?

She shook her head, moving quickly into the bedroom, unpacking the few things from her case, hanging the contentious suit away in the wardrobe. Anything to rid her mind of the insidious thought that had Jonas not left the country so precipitately she might have been tempted to go back to him.

She had changed into jeans and a sweater and was drinking a cup of coffee in the kitchen when she heard the outer door of the flat open and close and guessed, with a tightening of her nerves, that Angela was back. She must have seen Julie's sheepskin coat hanging in the hall because she came through to the living-room calling: 'Julie! Julie! Where are you?'

'I'm here.' Julie came out of the kitchen, finding a smile.

'Julie!' Angela hugged her closely, always affectionate, and Julie appreciated the other girl's warmth of greeting even though she had not expected to do so. 'How long have you been here?' Angela stood away from her, sensing that in spite of Julie's unchanged appearance something was troubling her. 'Is anything wrong?'

'Heavens, no!' Julie forced a light laugh. 'It's wonderful to be back in civilized surroundings again.'

Angela relaxed. 'Well, it's certainly good to see you again, darling. The flat's been like a tomb this past week. I've spent almost every evening out. I even went to see your mother.' She removed her coat to reveal a slim-fitting suit of beige wool. She always looked elegant, no matter what she wore. 'Well, tell me – did you get the interview?'

'Yes, I got it.' Julie turned back into the kitchen, not wanting Angela to see her face. 'What have you been doing?'

Angela came after her. 'This and that.' She frowned. 'Julie, has something happened? You seem – I don't know – distraught.'

Julie schooled her features and turned to look at her friend. 'No. What could have happened? It was a – shock, seeing Jonas again, naturally.'

'Naturally.' Angela nodded impatiently. 'Julie, you should have let me come with you. It's taken so long. I knew you'd hate it. Did he refuse to see you after bringing you all that way or something?'

'No, nothing like that. Actually – actually he had an accident while I was there. He cut his hand rather badly. It sort of – held things up.'

'Serves him right,' remarked Angela callously. 'Making you travel all that way. I saw Mark Bernstein. I told him exactly what I thought of him for forcing you into doing such a thing!'

Julie pressed a hand to her throat. 'And – and what did he say?'

Angela shrugged. 'I don't remember. Something about you being the only one for the job, all that twaddle. Anyway, it's over now, so we can return to normal. Have you had dinner?'

'What? Oh – no, not yet.'

'Let's eat out!' Angela spread her hands. 'A sort of celebration, eh?'

'Oh, really, I don't think so, Angela.' Julie could not face the thought of tackling a huge meal. 'I – I'd really rather just have an omelette or something here.'

Angela looked disappointed. 'But I'd treat you.'

'I'm not awfully hungry, honestly.' Julie made a dismissing gesture. 'But you go out, Angela. I don't mind.'

'Without you? Of course not.' Angela's mouth straightened. 'All right, we'll have omelettes here. And then afterwards we'll go round and see your mother, hmm?'

Julie shook her head. 'Not tonight, Angela. I'm rather tired, too. It's a long journey.'

Now why had she omitted to say that she had spent last night at Jonas's mother's house? For the same reasons she had not as yet admitted to staying at the castle ...

On Sunday, Julie could not avoid going out to Hampstead to see her mother. It was a fine, almost warm day, the kind that sometimes occurs in October and attempts to deceive the population into thinking that winter is still a long way off. She and Angela drove over in the morning in Julie's Mini and found her mother busy in the garden.

Mrs. Preston was a keen but meticulous gardener, and as a child Julie had found the formal lawns and flowerbeds more of a nuisance than anything. She remembered she had constantly been getting into trouble for walking on the new shoots or allowing her ball to knock the heads off the daffodils, and on one particular occasion she had suffered a week's detention in her room after school for falling and trying to save herself by dragging up one of her mother's prize rose trees. It had seemed an innocent offence to warrant such punishment, but Mrs. Preston had been adamant. The contrast between her mother and Mrs. Hunter, who Julie could never imagine treating a child in such a way, was all the more marked this morning after her recent stay at Howard's Green. She felt rather uncharitable, too, after her mother greeted her warmly and insisted that they both stay for lunch.

Over the meal, Julie repeated the information she had given Angela, and then came the question she had dreaded most.

'And where did you stay, dear?'

Julie swallowed the piece of meat she had been chewing and reached for her glass of wine. 'As a matter of fact, I stayed – at the castle,' she said, and waited for the explosion.

As she had half expected, it was Angela who reacted first. 'The castle? Jonas's castle? You stayed at *Jonas's* castle?' she gasped disbelievingly. 'But you didn't mention that when we were discussing it last evening!'

'How could you, Julie?' That was her mother, her lips curled fastidiously. 'How could you be so incredibly foolish?'

Julie knew her cheeks were turning scarlet. 'I don't know why you're both behaving as though some crime has been committed!' she exclaimed. 'It – it was perfectly respectable. He has a married couple – the Macphersons – living in. They looked after the place for his grandmother when she was alive.'

'It was his grandmother's castle?' asked her mother, frowning.

'Yes. But I never met her. She was too old at the time – at the time we got married, and as the castle was expected to pass to his uncle he never mentioned it.'

'And why didn't it?' asked Angela coldly. 'Pass to his uncle, I mean?'

'Oh! He – he died. He was killed in an air crash.'

'How convenient!' Angela looked at Mrs. Preston, tight-lipped.

Julie sighed. 'Well, it was just as well I could stay – at

the castle. There — there weren't any hotels in the area, and any guest-houses there had been were closed for the winter.'

'Well, I think you behaved irresponsibly, spending any time with that man,' said her mother bitterly. 'I'm quite sure he could have made other arrangements if he'd chosen to.' She fixed her daughter with a piercing stare. 'What happened between you?'

Julie strove to remain calm. They knew nothing — nothing.

'At — at the castle?' she ventured, playing for time. She had nothing to hide about her stay at the castle, and they need never know of that brief interlude at Howard's Green.

'Of course.' Angela was irritable.

Julie looked from one to the other of them feeling curiously alienated. She sensed their hostility, their feeling of betrayal, and she couldn't altogether blame them. They had not wanted her to go to Scotland, and by insisting on going she had aroused their resentment and impatience. But this was much worse. She was now admitting to fraternizing with the enemy, and no amount of justification would entirely exonerate her in their eyes. Were they not taking it all so seriously, it could have been farcical, thought Julie without humour.

'Nothing happened,' she said now. 'I — I had a job to do, and I did it. What makes you think Jonas would want anything to do with me after the way I've treated him?'

'After the way you've treated him!' echoed her mother in horror. 'What did he expect? Seducing your best friend!'

Julie pushed her plate aside. 'Let's not begin a discussion on that, Mother, please,' she appealed quietly. 'It's over now. All I've got to do is type out my notes.

Mark should be delighted.'

Angela looked as though she would have liked to have said more, but as luck would have it the vicar arrived a few minutes later to request Mrs. Preston's help in the forthcoming Christmas fair, and he stayed until the two girls were ready to leave.

But back at the flat, Angela gave full vent to her anger.

'You must have been out of your mind, Julie!' she exclaimed furiously. 'Putting yourself into his power – providing him with a heaven-sent opportunity!'

'A heaven-sent opportunity?' Julie's lips trembled. 'I – I told you, he didn't touch me—'

'Oh, not that!' Angela flung herself into an armchair. 'I know you better than that, I hope. I'm pretty sure you'd never let him lay his hands on you again.' Julie turned away so that her face should not betray her again, but Angela didn't notice. 'No—' she went on, 'I'm talking about divorce!'

'Divorce?' Julie felt hopelessly confused. 'I don't understand—'

'Your divorce, Julie!' explained Angela shortly. 'The divorce you should have insisted upon at the outset.'

'But what has—'

'Can't you see?' Angela's mouth was a thin line. 'Julie, you stayed at the castle. No court of law would grant you a divorce if Jonas could prove that, and he can, if he has these two old retainers to back him up.'

Julie didn't know why she should feel such an immense sense of relief. The question of the divorce had been weighing heavily on her mind, but now it seemed she had to make no immediate decision.

'Well, does it matter?' she murmured, bending to pick up a magazine, shaking a cushion, anything to avoid sitting down and becoming the cynosure of Angela's attention.

'Does it matter?' Angela was incredulous. 'Of course it matters, Julie. So long as you're still married to him, he's got a hold over you, and I don't like it.'

'I don't see how it affects you, Angela, one way or the other,' said Julie quietly.

Angela stared up at her, her eyes wide and accusing. 'You don't see how it affects me? Oh, Julie, you know I'm only thinking of you. I'm very fond of you. I don't want to see you getting hurt again.'

'I – I shan't—'

'You don't know what ideas Jonas Hunter may have. This whole thing may have been engineered by him to get you back again. And then what? More unfaithfulness – more humiliation!'

Julie shook her head. 'Angela, I'm sorry if I sound – well – indifferent, but the situation is no different now from what it was before I went away.'

But it is, a small voice inside her taunted.

However, much to her relief, Angela seemed to decide she had said enough for the present. She was still far from satisfied with her explanations, Julie could tell that, but for the moment she was prepared to let it go. Instead, she began telling Julie what had been happening that week at the salon, and later Julie got out her notes on Jonas and edited them ready for typing.

Going into the office on Monday morning, Julie began to feel a little more normal. This was her environment, and she had always been able to gain an immense amount of satisfaction from her work. She had her own small sanctum off the main office, and she knew her position was envied by more than one member of the staff. But her work was good, consistently so, and the enthusiasm she had always felt for it showed in the bright, co-ordinated style of her writing. It was through her enthusiasm to be successful that she had first met Jonas Hunter . . .

She had always wanted to write. She had dreamed of working for a national newspaper, interviewing people, covering important events, being on the spot when something momentous happened. But it hadn't been easy. National newspapers had their pick of applicants, many of them experienced, and one small girl with only her talent to commend her could not expect to get far. Interviews came and went and she was no nearer her goal than she had ever been.

So, using her own initiative, she started covering events on her own account, writing up stories and sending them in. Nothing happened to begin with. So far as she was aware the articles all ended up in someone's waste bin. But her persistence paid off. Six months later, one of her pieces fell into the hands of Jonas Hunter and recognizing the talent inherent in everything she wrote he asked to see any more that were sent in. Unaware of this, Julie carried on, gradually becoming more and more despondent, until one afternoon a sleek grey Aston Martin drew up outside her mother's house and a tall dark stranger came to the door.

Looking back on it now it was hard to remember the tremendous thrill she had felt when he had introduced himself. Jonas Hunter was almost a household name as far as she was concerned, and her mother, who for weeks had been protesting that Julie must get herself a proper job, was suitably impressed. He was invited into the splendid isolation of the parlour, which was seldom used by anyone but the vicar, and offered tea, which he declined. Julie had wondered what he must have thought of them, but afterwards Jonas had always maintained that from the very beginning he had been conscious of very little but the eager intelligence in a pair of wide-spaced hazel eyes.

Later, of course, after Julie was installed at the *Herald*, albeit in a very junior capacity, he began to notice other things about her. At that time his work was mainly free-lance, and he had had plenty of time to pick her up from work and take her home, sometimes offering her dinner, sometimes not. Julie was warned — she lost count of the number of times she was warned — not to have anything to do with him, that he was a wolf, that he ate little girls like her for breakfast, or perhaps supper was nearer the mark. He had the kind of reputation calculated to deter the most hardened matrons from offering their daughters in the matrimonial stakes even though his good looks and his social position encouraged them to try. He had escorted all the most sought-after models and debutantes at one time or another, but he remained dishearteningly unattached.

Julie knew all this, she had thought she was tempting fate having anything to do with him, and certainly her mother and Angela had not approved even then. But she hadn't been able to help herself. He did nothing to arouse any unwelcome suspicions in her mind, and their conversations were always interesting and impersonal. He was a fascinating raconteur, and she could sit for hours listening to him talking about the places he had visited. He could make the drabbest situations sound exciting, and if he sometimes took her hand in his enthusiasm and stroked it almost absentmindedly with his fingers she had not to imagine that he meant anything by it. All the same, those hand-holding sessions disturbed Julie more than she cared to admit, but if they left a restaurant and his fingers closed round her wrist she always managed to detach herself without too much difficulty.

For three months they saw one another almost every

day. She got to know him very well. He told her about his parents, and his brothers, and their home in Yorkshire, and she took him home to Hampstead on occasions, much to Mrs. Preston's annoyance. Her mother's initial reactions to Jonas had soon given way to anxiety concerning the possible effect he might have on Julie, nurtured, Julie had to admit, by Angela's gossip. She accepted that they meant well, but they didn't know Jonas as well as she did.

Then one week-end he asked her to go to Yorkshire with him, to meet his family. Julie had been eager to go until she got home and told her mother. Mrs. Preston of course thought the worst. She asked Julie whether Jonas's mother had offered the invitation or whether Jonas had relayed it to her. Naturally Julie had had to admit that she had not spoken to Mrs. Hunter, and from that moment on Mrs. Preston was convinced that he had no intention of taking her to his parents' home. She had pleaded with Julie not to go, but Julie, in spite of the fact that her nerves were on edge by this time, had refused to change her mind.

They had driven north in the evening, and if Jonas had noticed Julie's preoccupation with her thoughts he had made no comment. But the car had broken down on a lonely moorland road and suddenly everything her mother had suggested had become agonizingly possible.

Jonas, unaware of her suspicions, had suggested they make their way to the nearest farmhouse and ask for assistance, but Julie had refused to go with him. She had insisted on staying in the car, even though the moorland road was dark and unfamiliar, and she had seen by the hardening of his expression that he had correctly divined her thoughts. He had returned some time later with a garage mechanic who had quickly fixed the faulty carburettor and got the powerful engine started again. They had driven on in silence and although Julie had felt terrible about suspecting him she had not been able to bring herself to apologize.

They had arrived at Howard's Green as the family were sitting down to dinner. Nicholas and Paul had both been at home at that time and their welcome had increased her sense of contrition. However, Jonas gave her no opportunity to say anything more about it that evening. He had taken his father and brothers off to the village pub after the meal, leaving Julie to talk to his mother.

From the beginning Julie had liked Mrs. Hunter. They had got along well together, and if the older woman sensed that all was not well between her eldest son and the girl he had brought for the week-end she was discreet enough not to mention it. Julie was in bed by the time the men got back and it was not until after breakfast next morning that she had seen Jonas alone.

Mrs. Hunter had suggested he take Julie for a walk, to see something of the countryside, and as it was a pleasant September morning he had agreed. They had put on anoraks over slacks and sweaters and climbed the grassy slopes of Lonsdale Fell. Julie was searching for a way to bring up her stupidity of the night before when her foot had gone down a rabbit hole and she had cried out in agony as she lost her balance and collapsed on to the moist turf. Jonas had been beside her in a minute, going down on his haunches, taking her ankle between his long fingers, examining it for possible fractures. Julie had sat helplessly watching him, aware that she wanted his hands on her body, not just on her ankle, shocked that she should be experiencing such wanton thoughts.

He had looked up and encountered her eyes upon him, and his thin handsome face had hardened as it had done the previous evening. 'I'm surprised you came out with me alone after yesterday,' he had said harshly. 'Aren't you afraid I might take advantage of you? Foolish mouse! Do you think you could stop me if I chose to make love to you?'

Julie had shaken her head. 'I – I wish you would,' she had murmured unsteadily, and seen the glitter that entered his eyes.

'What did you say?' he had demanded. But Julie could not have repeated it. And of course, she didn't have to. Jonas lowered his weight beside her, cupping her face in his hands, bending his head and putting gentle lips to her quivering mouth.

It was the first time he had kissed her, and apart from the boyish caresses she had experienced in her schooldays, Julie had little experience to draw on. But her lips had parted almost involuntarily and the kiss which had begun as such a tentative caress hardened and lengthened into passion. Jonas had borne her back against the springy softness of the turf and kissed her until she was weak and clinging to him. Then he had dragged himself away, torn up a blade of grass and said: 'I want to make love to you, and I'm not accustomed to denying myself anything I want, as no doubt you've heard. But in this instance it's rather different. I think I'm in love with you. How's that for a laugh!'

This speech was delivered in a low, impassioned tone, and Julie was unable to understand why he should sound so angry about something that filled her with an overwhelming feeling of delight. A few moments ago she could have denied him nothing, she had realized that. In spite of all the warnings she had had, in spite of her respect for her mother and Angela, if Jonas had chosen to make love to her she would not have been able to stop him. That was why it was so wonderful that he had been the one to draw back. She pulled herself upright, her hand on his shoulder, and he turned to look at her, his eyes darkened by his emotions.

'Oh, Julie!' he muttered thickly, 'don't look at me like that! I'm not worth it. I'm too old for you – you're just starting out on your career and you can't possibly be expected to understand this selfish need I have to make you belong to me, to possess you – your body as well as your mind.' He stroked a strand of chestnut hair blown by the wind from her lips. 'I've tried to show you these past months that I'm not entirely the selfish brute I have the reputation of being, but last night – when you began to doubt me—' He shook his head. 'I wanted to hurt you, Julie. But I can't. *I can't*.' He looked away from her. 'You see what a fool you've made of me!'

'Oh, Jonas!' She buried her face against his shoulder, sliding her arm through his, clinging to him, glorying in the power he had given her. 'I – I'm sorry. I listened to my mother. She was convinced you had no intention of – of bringing me to meet your parents.'

Jonas looked sideways at her. 'Oh, I see.' He frowned. 'And you?'

Julie held his gaze with her own. 'I've always believed in you, Jonas.'

He smiled, and it was a miraculous transformation of his features. 'Oh, Julie!' he muttered huskily. 'What am I going to do with you?'

'What would you like to do?'

'You know what I want,' he answered quietly.

Julie swallowed hard. 'All – all right.'

'All right – what?'

'All right – have me!'

His eyes narrowed. 'Exactly what are you talking about?'

For a moment he had frightened her and she had stared at him almost tremulously. 'I – I thought – that is, you said you wanted to – to make love to me . . .'

'I do.'

Julie trembled. 'Well then—'

'Well then, what?' He shook his head. 'Oh, Julie, you crazy little fool! Did you think I was suggesting we should sleep together? Did you think that was what I wanted – what I was denying myself?'

'W-wasn't it?' She was totally confused now.

'No.' He cupped her chin with one hand. 'I would like to marry you. You know – wedding bells, orange blossom, the whole scene!'

Julie couldn't believe it. She stared at him and the hot tears had overflowed her eyes and trickled unheeded down her cheeks. For weeks she had steeled herself not to read anything into his casual companionship, had avoided physical contact with him for fear of giving her futile emotions away. And now . . .

Jonas had looked down at her uncomprehendingly, licking the salty drops from her lips, unable to prevent himself from opening those lips again and seeking the warmth from within.

'Why are you crying, Julie?' he had asked at last, and she had told him. Because she was in love with him, too, because she cared too deeply for him ever to consider the difference in their ages any disadvantage, because she had never been so happy in her life . . .

And they had been happy, that was the amazing thing. Their relationship had expanded and developed, they explored each other's minds and each other's bodies with equal urgency, and at no time had Julie ever imagined he would betray her as he had done.

CHAPTER NINE

JULIE was typing out the notes on the interview when Mark sent for her.

Mark Bernstein's office was vastly different from her own – thick grey carpet, panelled walls, leather-surfaced desk, and a view over half of London. The man himself dominated the office, however – not very tall, but stocky, with greying black hair, beetling brows and a thick Mexican-style moustache. She knew he was forty-five and unmarried, and that her position here was secured by his genuine liking for her, but there had never been anything remotely intimate between them. He welcomed her warmly, settled her into the leather chair opposite his own, and rang through to his secretary and ordered coffee for two.

'Now,' he said, sitting down and reaching for one of the chunky cigars he smoked. 'What happened?'

Julie sighed. 'I got the interview.'

'You did?' Mark was delighted. 'That's marvellous!'

'I'm in the process of deciphering my notes at the moment. When do you want it?'

'There's no hurry. I've got that piece on Sarah Ardley to go in this week. You know – the general's wife who writes those ghastly science fiction things.'

Julie nodded, and there was a tap at the door and the secretary came in with the tray of coffee. She left it on the desk beside Julie and she took charge of it, glad of the diversion. As she poured Mark's, however, his expression changed and he said: 'You're looking very pale, Julie. How did it really go?'

Julie pushed his coffee towards him. 'I don't know what you mean.'

'Yes, you do. Julie, this man is still your husband. I'm not without some sensibilities. I can appreciate the difficulties involved.'

'Can you?' Julie sounded sceptical.

'Yes.' Mark drew impatiently on his cigar. 'And I have to tell you – Hunter asked for the interview himself. He – he forced my hand.'

Julie looked at him sympathetically, realizing what it must have cost him to tell her that. 'I know.'

'You *know*?'

'Yes, Jonas told me.' She sipped her coffee. 'Hmm, this is good. Better than the machine in the office.'

Mark ignored her. 'Julie, why did he do it? What did he want? I mean, I'd hate to think I'd been responsible for – well, causing you any more unhappiness.' He shook his head. 'Angela fairly bit my head off when I saw her.'

Julie put down her cup. 'Angela doesn't like Jonas.'

'Doesn't she? I always used to think she fancied him herself.' He shook his head. 'I was probably wrong. And you're a grown woman, Julie. You can make your own decisions.'

'Yes.' Julie forced a smile. 'They're not always the right ones, though.'

'No?' Mark gave a rueful smile. 'But you can be pretty pigheaded when you choose to be.' He tapped ash into the onyx tray. 'By the way, there's an assignment coming up which I think might appeal to you. One of these mid-European principalities, you know the sort of place? Well, there's to be a wedding . . .'

The remainder of the interview was taken up with discussing Julie's possible trip to Europe, and when she returned to her office she was glad to have something new to think about and plan for. While she was in the office she could occupy her mind. It was when she left it she felt that awful sense of desperation.

To make matters worse, when she left work that evening and went out to the car park to start her car, the Mini refused to fire. Most of her colleagues had already left and rather than spend useless minutes looking into the engine she locked the doors again and went to find a taxi. She would phone the garage when she got home and have them pick it up and repair it. It was probably nothing too serious.

It wasn't easy getting a taxi at that hour of the evening, but at last she managed to summon one and scrambled inelegantly into the back before an elderly businessman could beat her to it. She gave her address and sat back with relief. In the matter of engaging taxis, women's rights were far less than equal!

It didn't take long to reach Pallister Court and she paid the driver and ran lightly up the steps to the door. As she did so, the sleek lines of a sports saloon caught her eye. It was parked in the small area to one side of the entrance where she usually kept her Mini, and she could almost swear it was a Porsche, Jonas's Porsche . . .

She chided herself angrily for being a fool. She had Jonas Hunter on the brain. Even if it was a Porsche, there must be dozens of them in London. And in any case, why would he be here? Unless . . . Her pulses quickened. Unless he had come to see her . . . or Angela . . .

Her palms were moist as she climbed the stairs to the first floor landing, and there was an awful feeling of unease probing at the nerves in her stomach so that she felt almost sick with anticipation.

She heard the voices as soon as she opened the door to the flat, angry voices that had clearly not overheard her entrance. She had intended to call out: 'Angela! I'm home!' anything to make her presence known; but she couldn't help recognizing that one of the voices was Jonas's, and that silenced her. She was not an eavesdropper, she had never listened in to other people's conversations before. But there was something so hostile about the argument that was taking place in the living-room that when she heard her name mentioned she froze into immobility.

'Julie will never believe you!' That was Angela, her voice strident and scornful.

'I wouldn't be too sure of that.' That, of course, was Jonas. He sounded angry, too, but he didn't have to raise his voice to command a hearing. 'I don't think she's properly considered what this means.'

'She never will—'

'I think she might. If I ask her.' Jonas uttered an imprecation. 'What did you do that for?'

Angela laughed, and it was not a pleasant sound. 'You made me. You can't keep away from me. When Julie comes back she'll see for herself that you've been up to your old tricks.'

'I could kill you for that, Angela!'

Julie's heart almost stopped beating at the menace in his voice. What was going on here? What were they arguing about? And what had Angela done?

Angela laughed again. 'You wouldn't do that, Jonas. You wouldn't dare!'

'Oh, I'd dare all right,' muttered Jonas savagely, and Julie's hand reached for the handle of the living-room door. She could not let this go on. But before she could reveal herself he went on: 'But I have no intention of making a martyr of you, Angela! Julie has to see you as you really are – mean and jealous – and sick!'

'Sick?'

'Yes, sick, Angela. Only a sick mind could have dreamed up that scheme. But you overstepped the mark, didn't you? Julie coming back like that almost threw you, didn't it? I often wondered how you managed to get your clothes off and get into the bed in time. You couldn't possibly have planned it, and as Julie wasn't expected home that morning I could see no reason for staging such a charade without an audience. I didn't know about the letter, of course. Julie never told me. Which was lucky for you. But then it all turned out well so far as you were concerned, didn't it? You had only to appeal to Julie's sensitivity – play on her sympathies – trade on her believing you because you'd always pretended I wasn't good enough for her!'

'You're not!' Angela almost screamed the words.

'You're jealous, Angela. Jealous of what Julie and I shared. Jealous – because you wanted it yourself!'

'Don't flatter yourself—'

'Oh, I'm not. But I am aware you'd have done anything to separate us. That was why I left the country. I couldn't bear to see Julie being deceived and not being able to do anything about it.' He uttered an oath. 'God, if I'd known about that letter—'

'But you didn't did you, Jonas?'

Julie blinked, trying to think coherently. They had to be talking about the anonymous letter she had received, but how did Jonas know about that? Then she remembered. She had told his mother. Mrs. Hunter must have telephoned her son and told him. But why? What difference did the letter make? And why was Jonas so furious because he hadn't known about it? It only confirmed what she had seen with her own eyes – confirmed that someone else had known about their affair . . .

She swallowed convulsively, hot colour staining her cheeks. But what was it Angela had said about that awful night? That Jonas had taken her out – given her too much to drink – and seduced her . . . Julie drew an uneven breath. That still stuck in her throat no matter how she tried to ignore the implications. But anyway, Angela had insisted that there had been only this one occasion. She had said that in the past she had always refused to have anything to do with him. She had been the innocent party to his deception and had been shattered when Julie found out what had happened.

Julie sagged. But even that proved nothing. The letter must have been false, but so what? People were always trying to cause trouble. Her spirits plummeted. She simply could not understand why Jonas should have considered the letter so important. It was still Jonas's word against Angela's, and even after what she had just heard she could not believe he was entirely innocent.

Angela was speaking again, and despising herself for listening Julie pressed her finger tips against her lips.

'—and anyway, Julie is hardly likely to pay any attention to you, with the marks of another woman's nails scored on your cheek. She'll be home soon. I always hear her car coming into the yard. The silencer is cracked, you know. I wonder what she'll say when she finds you here—'

Suddenly, without any warning, the living-room door was wrenched open and Julie stared agonizingly into Jonas's shocked face. As Angela had said, there were scratches on his face, and she had made them.

'*Julie!*' He sounded stunned. 'My God, how long have you been there?'

'Julie – Julie, is that you?' Angela came pushing past Jonas into the small hallway, looking anxiously at Julie's pale face. 'Oh, Julie, thank heavens you've come! Jonas has been here for ages—'

'Fifteen minutes, to be exact!' stated Jonas quietly, but Angela contradicted him scornfully.

'He's been here much longer than that, Julie. I don't know why he came. He knows I want nothing more to do with him—'

Jonas cast a savage look at her and then grasped Julie firmly by the shoulders, giving her a little shake. 'Julie! Stop looking as though you've seen a ghost! I want to know – how long have you been here?'

'Wh-why—'

Angela broke in on them. 'He wants to reassure himself that you haven't overheard the things he's been saying to me,' she exclaimed spitefully. 'He came in here, demanding that I tell you that everything I said before was lies, all lies! As if I could! When I refused, he started shaking me and I scratched his face—'

'I was here when you scratched his face,' said Julie slowly, almost uncomprehendingly.

Angela was clearly taken aback. 'You – were – here—'

'Were you, Julie, were you?' Jonas was staring desperately at her, his lean cheek livid where Angela's long nails had scored their path. Julie felt nauseated by the image that created, and she drew back from him so that his hands dropped to his sides.

'Yes,' she replied unsteadily, 'I was here. I've gathered that your mother told you about the letter—'

'Yes. Yes, she did. Julie, if you were here, you must have realized—'

Angela interposed herself between them. 'Darling, forget about it. It's all over and done with. Surely the fact that Jonas came here today with the intention of forcing me into lying for his sake proves that he's been deceiving

164

you all along . . .' She put an arm around Julie's shoulders, but the other girl flinched away from her, too. 'Julie, Julie dear! Come along inside. You look ghastly. Where have you been anyway? I didn't hear the car.'

'It wouldn't start. I took a cab.' Julie answered her automatically. Then she turned to Jonas again. She had to know the truth, whatever it cost her. What did that letter mean to him? 'Jonas, what did you mean when you said you wished you'd known about the letter at the time?'

'Because Angela sent that letter,' stated Jonas grimly.

Julie took a backward step. 'What?'

'Don't take any notice of him, Julie,' exclaimed Angela forcefully. 'What possible reason could I have for sending you such a letter? Good heavens, I had no need of letters. We're friends. We've always *told* one another everything. You know that!' She sounded reproachful.

Julie had listened to what she had to say, but then she looked at Jonas again. 'Well, Jonas?' she said, forcing her voice not to tremble. 'That's true, isn't it?'

Jonas's expression was contemptuous. 'You think so?'

'What do you mean?'

'I've told you, Julie, he came here to cause trouble—'

Jonas ignored Angela's outburst and went on: 'You're forgetting something, Julie. You weren't expected back until the evening of that day. Even Angela could never have dreamed of having the good luck to have you come back unexpectedly and find her at the apartment. She had to be sure you knew, and what better way than by sending a letter? Who else would have done such a thing?'

'I – I don't know—' Julie didn't know what to think. 'But even if I hadn't come back, I would never have been sure—'

'Oh, you would. Angela would have seen to that.'

'You're not making any ground here, Jonas!' Angela was contemptuous now. She knew Julie was hurt and confused and she took advantage of it. 'Everything you're saying has been said before. Julie doesn't believe you. She knows the kind of man you are.'

'What kind of man am I, Angela?' His voice was dangerously soft.

'The kind of man who would seduce your wife's best friend without giving it a second thought—'

'Why, you—'

Jonas took a step forward, but now Julie interposed herself between them. 'This has gone far enough, Jonas,' she said wearily. 'I accept that there might be more to this than I originally thought, and that you despise Angela for what she's supposed to have done—'

'You still believe her?' Jonas was incredulous.

'I – I don't know.' Julie shook her head, unable to forget Angela's shrill voice as she hurled insults at him, the way she had deliberately scratched his cheek. 'I don't know what I believe any more.'

'Oh, for God's sake!'

Jonas thrust her roughly aside and strode out of the flat, slamming the door behind him. After he had gone, Julie felt utterly bereft. She grasped the door handle for support as everything began to revolve at an ever-increasing pace. She had the distinct feeling that she was losing contact with the world and her eyes blurred. Angela sensed what was happening to her. She grasped the back of her neck and pushed Julie's head downwards, forcing the blood into her aching brain. The faintness receded and drawing away from Angela she brushed past her into the living-room. She still felt sick and ill, and the last person she felt she wanted helping her at this time was

Angela.

The other girl followed her into the room and once Julie was sitting on the settee, she said: 'I'm going to make some tea. You look as though you need some.'

Julie made no protest and with an impatient look at her to assure herself that she was all right, Angela left her.

When she came back, Julie had not moved, and Angela clicked her tongue. 'Julie, for heaven's sake, take off your coat and stop looking so – so tragic! He's gone. And somehow I don't think he'll be coming back.'

Julie dragged her eyes up to meet the other girl's. 'I know that. But I may go after him.'

'*What?*' Angela was astounded.

'You heard what I said, Angela. I think you ought to know – I still love Jonas, no matter what he did.'

'You idiot!' Angela was furious. 'You can't be serious!'

'Why not?' Julie moved her shoulders. 'It's the truth. I think I've known it all along, only I let you and Mother persuade me otherwise. And then, with Jonas leaving the country ...'

'But you couldn't go back to him, Julie. There've probably been other women—'

'I've discovered that I don't particularly care any more, Angela. I don't have a lot of pride where he's concerned. What is it they say about half a loaf being better than no bread?'

Angela uttered an expletive. 'You're a fool, Julie. Just because you've spent a few days in his company you're deceiving yourself into thinking you can go back and live with him! What will you do if he gets bored with you? Form a *menage à trois?*'

Julie's stomach contracted. 'That's a horrible thing to

say, Angela. Why can't you accept that Jonas is the only man for me? I can't be hard and sophisticated like you. I love Jonas!'

'You think I'm hard and sophisticated, do you?' Angela's mouth turned down at the corners. 'Just because I have more sense than to make a doormat of myself for any man? Men are exploiters, Julie, and it's up to us as women to exploit them first!'

Julie shook her head. 'I don't see things like that,' she insisted quietly. 'I'm married to Jonas, and as you pointed out yesterday that gives us some sort of a hold over one another. At least we might try to start again—'

'And you think he'll let you?'

'I don't know. That's something I have to find out.'

'How do you know that this isn't what he's wanted all along? For you to go crawling back to him so that he can grind you under his heel.'

Julie flinched. 'I've thought of that, of course. But I've got to take that chance.'

Angela stared at her with dislike. 'You are a fool, Julie. You really are. I didn't recognize it until now, but you're truly stupid.'

Julie got to her feet. 'I don't have to listen to that kind of talk from you, Angela—'

'Don't you? Don't you just?' Angela's composure was beginning to crack. 'And what if I told you I'd been lying all along? That it was Jonas who was telling the truth all these years? That nothing happened between us? What would you do then?'

Julie stared at her aghast. 'Are – are you telling me that, Angela?'

Angela shrugged. 'Why not? Why should I lie about it any longer? If you're prepared to take the swine back anyway.'

'But – but why—'

'Why did I do it, you mean? Surely you've realized. My God, Jonas has known for years.'

'Known what?' Julie still couldn't take it in.

'I wanted Jonas Hunter, Julie. It's as simple as that. And I'd have had him too if you hadn't started writing those articles to the paper and aroused his curiosity.'

'You mean – you mean you knew him – before—'

'Of course. He had a girl-friend who came to the salon. That was how I met him.'

'But – but you never told me—'

'Why should I? Seeing you with him made me sick to my stomach!'

'Oh, Angela!'

Julie realized she actually had it in her heart to feel sorry for the other girl. But where did it leave her?

Angela was turning away. 'Well, go, can't you?' she muttered violently. 'Go to your precious Jonas, and good luck to you! And just for the record, I did send that letter. You've no idea what satisfaction your separation gave me.'

'*Angela!*'

'*Go!* Go away. Get out of my sight.'

Angela gave her one last contemptuous glance and Julie went, snatching up her handbag in the hall, and hurrying own the stairs as fast as her legs would carry her. But she had no idea where she was going.

CHAPTER TEN

JULIE stared blindly through the taxi windows, unable to recognize her surroundings even now. It was too dark, and the rain that was driving against them constricted visibility. But it couldn't be too much farther, she realized, not without some misgivings, and wondered again whether she had been foolish in coming here. But there had seemed nowhere else to go ...

She caught her lower lip tightly between her teeth. Thank goodness she had had the sense to pick up her handbag as she left the flat. Without it, she would have had to resort to the ignominious humiliation of having to ask for assistance from Mark Bernstein, or another of her working colleagues. As it was, she had had just enough to pay her fare to Darlington and a little over for the taxi to take her to Howard's Green.

She drew her coat collar closer about her throat. It was late, after eleven, and Mrs. Hunter might well be in bed. And if she was, would she have the courage to waken her? She would have to. She could hardly stand about in the pouring rain till morning.

She shivered. But what reason had she to suppose that Mrs. Hunter would welcome her here? When she had heard Julie's story might she not change her mind about that casually offered invitation? Might she not feel as Jonas would surely do that Julie deserved no sympathy after the way she had behaved? Oh, if only she had not been so gullible, so easily deceived; so willing to doubt where no doubt existed! She had been thinking of going after Jonas, as she had told Angela, but that was before she had learned the truth. After that, it had seemed impossible. To offer forgiveness, to offer a chance to start again with the mistakes of the past behind them – that was one thing. But to go to Jonas having learned the truth and expect him to forgive her – that was something else. In his position she felt she would never want to see her again.

And so she had run away, a cowardly thing to do, no doubt, but at least no one would think of looking for her here. She couldn't bear the thought of seeing Angela until she had had the chance to get things into perspective again, and to go to Hampstead, to confide in her mother to whom Angela had always behaved like a second daughter, was totally unacceptable.

The taxi was slowing and she saw the lights of the village glinting ahead of them.

'This is it, miss,' the driver was saying, peering at the houses that flanked the road. 'Where is this house you're going to?'

'It's through the village – on the outskirts.' Julie sat forward trying to ignore the quickened beating of her heart. 'Look, there it is! Can you see it? The one set back amongst the trees.'

The taxi driver nodded and turned between the gates. To Julie's relief there were lights in the downstairs rooms as on the evening Jonas had brought her here, and she clutched her handbag tightly. The taxi came to a halt at the steps and she paid the fare before thrusting open the door and scrambling out.

'Thank you,' she called, and the taxi driver gave her a brief nod before reversing expertly down the drive again.

Julie ran quickly up the steps to shelter under the canopy and rang the bell. It was some minutes before the door was tentatively opened, but when Mrs. Hunter saw who her visitor was she pulled the door wide.

'Julie!' she cried. 'What a surprise! Come along in. I couldn't think who might be calling at this time of night. Living alone, one tends to become rather cautious about opening one's door after nine o'clock.'

Julie stepped into the warm hallway, nodding apologetically. 'I – I'm sorry. I know it's late—'

Mrs. Hunter shook her head impatiently. 'Don't be silly, my dear. I don't mind. You know you're always welcome here. Come into the lounge and get your wet coat off. You look half frozen.'

Julie felt an enormous weight had been lifted from her shoulders. Her mother-in-law was so normal, so matter-of-fact; she might have been calling in the early evening instead of approaching midnight. She unfastened her coat and Mrs. Hunter draped it over the banister, then they went into the lounge.

'Now,' said Mrs. Hunter, ushering her visitor into a chair, 'are you hungry? Would you like something to eat?'

'Nothing to eat, thank you.' Julie forced a smile. 'I – er – I had something on the train.' That was an outright lie, but she didn't want to worry the older woman by behaving as sickly as she felt.

Mrs. Hunter frowned. 'Some coffee, then. Or tea?'

'No, really—'

'Well, I insist you have something,' declared her mother-in-law firmly. 'I know – some brandy. That will warm you up.'

Julie didn't argue and when the glass of amber-coloured liquid was placed in her hand she sipped it obediently. The raw spirit was warming and the heat it generated spread throughout her system. Her nerves relaxed and she felt a little better. Mrs. Hunter poured herself a glass of sherry and then seated herself opposite.

'Well,' she said with a smile, 'you've chosen a foul night to come calling.'

Julie nodded. 'It – it was raining in London.'

'Was it? You've travelled up from London this evening?'

'I came up by train, yes.'

'I see.' Mrs. Hunter looked down into her glass. 'Was this a sudden decision?'

Julie sighed. 'Very sudden.'

'I thought it might have been. You haven't brought any luggage. And you are going to stay, aren't you?' She looked up at her daughter-in-law piercingly.

Julie nodded again. 'If – if you'll have me.'

Mrs. Hunter looked exasperated. 'If I'll have you! Julie, you know you've always been welcome here. If in recent years we've seen nothing of one another, that hasn't been my fault.'

'I – I know that.'

'So.' Mrs. Hunter sipped her sherry. 'You look tired. I suggest you go upstairs when you've finished that, have a hot bath, and get into bed. I'll bring a hot drink up later. You look as though you could do with a few days' rest.'

Julie stared at her. 'But – but – don't you want to know why I've come?'

'Do you want to talk about it tonight?'

'I – not particularly. But I must.'

'Nonsense! We'll talk some other time. When you're rested – when you've stopped looking like a pale ghost of the girl I used to know.'

Julie's lips trembled 'You – you may not want me here when – when I tell you—'

Her mother-in-law shook her head. 'You may be my

son's wife, Julie, but you're also a person in your own right. And nothing you can say will alter my opinion of you. Now drink that up and I'll run your bath.'

'Oh, really—' Julie could feel the tears pricking at her eyes at the other woman's kindness. 'I – I can manage—'

'Leave everything to me,' said Mrs. Hunter firmly. 'You're in no fit state to argue!'

It was such a relief to do as she said, to take off her clothes and sink into the scented bath, washing away the stigma of that terrible scene at the flat. Then she put on a cotton nightdress belonging to Mrs. Hunter and slipped between the sheets of Paul's bed. There was a hot malted drink waiting for her and two aspirins lying on the bed-side table. Mrs. Hunter waved away her thanks and told her to settle down and get a good night's sleep.

Julie hadn't expected to sleep even so. She was sure that once she closed her eyes the events of the day would come crowding in on her. But surprisingly enough, they didn't. Instead, the warmth of the bed and the knowledge that for the present nothing else was demanded of her worked as a sedative could never do and she fell into a dreamless slumber and didn't wake until a watery sun was high in the sky.

She was lying there allowing awareness of her surroundings to creep over her when the bedroom door opened and Mrs. Hunter peeped in.

'Oh, you're awake!' she exclaimed with a smile.

'Umm.' Julie propped herself up on her elbows. 'I feel much better. I must have gone to sleep the minute my head touched the pillow.'

'That's good.' Her mother-in-law came further into the room. 'Well, it's nearly twelve o'clock. Do you want breakfast, or will you wait for lunch?'

Julie managed a smile. 'Heavens, I don't want any breakfast at this time!' She bit her lip. 'Thank you.'

Mrs. Hunter fussed about, tidying the coverlet, picking up one of Julie's boots and straightening it. 'Well, if you don't want breakfast, I'll bring you some coffee. I'm sure you won't say no to that.'

'I can get up,' Julie protested.

'You stay where you are,' directed Mrs. Hunter sternly. 'I won't be a minute. The kettle has boiled.'

She was back five minutes later with a tray set for two and seated herself on the end of the bed to drink hers. 'It's a fine morning,' she said. 'I've been out tidying up the garden. There are leaves everywhere.'

Julie drank the coffee. It was good, hot and strong, the way she liked it. The way Jonas liked it, too. Jonas . . .

'Nicholas and Joanne are coming for tea this afternoon,' her mother-in-law was going on. 'You'll see the baby. She's gorgeous, just sitting up and taking notice.'

Julie felt terrible. 'I – I can't stay here – not when they're coming,' she protested unsteadily.

'Why not? You've met Joanne, haven't you?'

'Once, I think. They – they weren't married when Jonas and I—' She broke off. 'Mrs. Hunter, Jonas doesn't know I'm here.'

'I had gathered that.' The older woman placed her empty cup on the tray. 'But that doesn't matter. Nicholas and Joanne seldom see Jonas anyway.'

'You don't understand . . . Julie heaved a sigh. 'I – I found out yesterday that – that Angela was lying, all along.'

Mrs. Hunter didn't look surprised. 'Ah! The letter, I suppose.'

'The letter? Oh! Oh, no, not really.' Julie bent her head. 'It's a long story and not a very pleasant one.'

'You don't have to talk about it now—'

'I do. I – I'd rather. I'd like you to know the facts.'

'All right.' Mrs. Hunter looked expectantly at her. 'Jonas came to your flat, didn't he?'

'How do you know that?'

'I rang him. I told him about the letter—'

'Yes, I guessed you had.'

'—and he said he was going to see you. To confront you with the fact that Angela must have sent it.'

'I – I see.'

'It had to be her. You see, Jonas could never understand why Angela did what she did. I mean, you know now that he was telling the truth, and that Angela really did go to the apartment?'

'Yes.'

'Well, he could never understand how she *knew* you would come back and find her. I mean, if you hadn't, all her efforts were for nothing. Unless she confessed – just like that. He guessed that she had sent the letter for you to find on your return and then some time she would let it drop that she'd been at the apartment while you were away, and – well, it isn't too difficult to imagine the kind of confession she'd have been prepared to make. But she had to have proof, real proof, that what she was saying had some basis in fact. That was why she needed to spend that night at the apartment. She knew you would never believe anything that couldn't be proved.'

Julie nodded, feeling sick again. 'I was a fool!'

Mrs. Hunter shrugged. 'Perhaps. But Angela did her work well, and you were always too easily influenced by your mother, weren't you?'

'I suppose so.'

Mrs. Hunter sighed. 'You don't have to pretend with me, Julie. I know your mother has never really liked

Jonas, but I know my son. He may have behaved irresponsibly in the past, but after you two were married he
never even looked at another woman. I know that. I
always knew that when he fell in love with someone it
would happen that way. He was very much like his
father, and goodness knows Godfrey had his moments.'
She broke off and pressed her lips together to compose
herself. Then she went on: 'When you walked out on him,
he was absolutely shattered. I think if his father hadn't
persuaded him to take that overseas appointment he'd
have had a complete breakdown.'

'And it was all my fault!' Julie felt terrible.

'Not at all. Angela Forrest was to blame. Jonas knew
she would cause trouble if she could. He'd known her
before, you see. She was madly jealous. She'd have done
anything to split you two up. Jonas knew that. But he
didn't know how to convince you when you thought so
well of her.'

Julie shook her head. 'I never knew about their association,' she said bitterly. 'If I had—'

'You'd have been jealous, too,' murmured Mrs. Hunter
sagely.

'Perhaps so.' Julie shook her head. 'But no longer.'

'So what happened?'

Julie hesitated for a moment and then she said: 'As
usual I was foolish. I was late home last night. My car
wouldn't start and I took a cab. Jonas was there when I
arrived at the flat. He was arguing with Angela. They
didn't hear me. I – I listened.' She plucked at the coverlet.
'I didn't want to. But I heard my name, and I couldn't
help myself.' She sighed heavily. 'Even then I didn't
grasp the full meaning behind what Angela was saying. It
was hard to understand, and I was so confused.' She made
a helpless gesture. 'I'm not excusing myself. I should have

gone into the room and demanded to know what was going on. But I didn't. I just stayed there like – like a mouse – and then Jonas came out and found me.' She shivered with the remembered agony of it all. 'He – he asked me how long I'd been there and Angela said it was because he was afraid I'd overheard what he'd been saying to her. She – she had scratched his cheek, you see, and it looked awful—'

'Angela had scratched his cheek?' echoed Mrs. Hunter incredulously.

'Yes, yes, I realize now why she did it. She wanted me to think he'd been bothering her again – that she'd had to fight him off. But at the time I was too stunned to think coherently.'

Mrs. Hunter's face was grim. 'Then what happened?'

Julie bent her head. 'Jonas – Jonas asked me whether in spite of everything I still believed Angela. I – I said I didn't know, and – and he just left. He walked out.'

'What did you expect?' Mrs. Hunter was ironic.

'Oh, I know. I don't blame him. I – I should have done the same, I suppose. But – but after he'd gone I started thinking that – that perhaps I'd been too hasty, that maybe we could still have a life together . . .'

'You mean you were prepared to accept his unfaithfulness?'

'I – I was prepared to try.'

'Oh, Julie! So why didn't you?' She paused. 'Or did you?'

Julie shook her head. 'No.' She drew a deep breath. 'I – I didn't feel very well, and Angela said she would make some tea. Then – then I said that I had realized I was still in love with Jonas and that I was thinking of going after him. She – she was furious!'

'I can imagine.' Mrs. Hunter's lips curled.

'Yes. Well, she said I would be a fool – that Jonas would never take me back.'

'But he would!'

'I was going to try anyway. Then – then she told me she'd been lying.'

Mrs. Hunter frowned. 'But surely you were relieved then. You sound so – so regretful, somehow.'

'I – I am. How can I go back to Jonas now – knowing the truth? It was different when I thought he was to blame. I wanted to show him I could forgive him—'

'And don't you think he'll forgive you?'

Julie stared helplessly at her. 'Do you think he will?'

'I'm sure of it.' Mrs. Hunter's lips were trembling a little. 'You were prepared to try again. Otherwise you would have never learned the truth.'

'But will he believe that? I'm afraid—'

'My son is not a man to bear grudges. And he loves you, Julie, I know he does. If you tell him it's so, he'll believe you.'

'Will he?' Julie pressed hands to her cheeks. 'You make me feel so – so petty after what's happened. Oh, if only I'd gone with him last night . . .'

'And never learned the truth? No?' Her mother-in-law patted her shoulder reassuringly. 'Well, it's over now. You've got the future to think about. And perhaps we should let Jonas know where you are—'

'*No!*' Julie caught her breath. 'No, don't do that.'

'Why not?'

'It – it wouldn't do any good. Mrs. Hunter, I'm very much afraid that so far as Jonas is concerned I don't matter any more . . .'

'What are you talking about?'

'That – that night we stayed here—'

'You slept together, I know.'

'You *know*?'

'Of course. Jonas told me. He didn't really get a phone call from London that morning. He told me what he'd done and that he despised himself for taking advantage of you—'

'Oh, *Jonas*!' Julie pressed her palms to her hot cheeks.

'I gather you took his departure to mean something else?'

Julie nodded, and Mrs. Hunter rose to her feet.

'Very well. You get up when you feel like it. I'm going to make a telephone call, right?'

'All right.' Julie moved her head slowly up and down. 'And – and Mrs. Hunter . . .'

'Yes?'

'I – I don't know how to thank you . . .'

'Don't try. Just make my son happy, hmm?'

When Julie went downstairs later, bathed and dressed, she found her mother-in-law working in the kitchen. She hesitated for a moment and then she had to say: 'Did – did you speak to Jonas?'

'No.' Mrs. Hunter looked up from slicing carrots. 'I'm afraid not.'

'Oh!' Julie swallowed convulsively. 'Why not?'

'I rang his apartment, but there was no reply.'

'I see.' Julie's hands curled into her palms. 'He – he must be out.'

'Yes.' Mrs. Hunter sounded impatient. 'That's a reasonable conclusion.'

Julie sighed. 'I'm sorry.' She looked round. 'Is there anything I can do?'

Mrs. Hunter hesitated and then she nodded. 'You can peel some potatoes, if you want to.' She paused. 'I'll ring again after lunch.'

Julie ate hardly any of the delicious meal her mother-in-law had prepared for her and waited expectantly for Mrs. Hunter to make the second call. But again there was no reply, and although Mrs. Hunter tried several times before Nicholas, Joanne and baby Penny arrived, she got no satisfaction.

Jonas's brother and his wife were surprised to see Julie, but they hid their curiosity and spoke to her in a friendly manner. The baby provided the necessary outlet for their embarrassment and Julie found her utterly en-chanting. It was perhaps fortunate that Penny took to this new auntie with equal enthusiasm, and with the baby on her knee Julie lost her nervous tension for a few hours.

'Do – do you see anything of Jonas these days, Julie?' asked Joanne over tea, eager to dispel any lingering sense of constraint.

Julie popped a finger of sponge into Penny's small mouth before replying. 'As – as a matter of fact—' she was beginning, when Mrs. Hunter took pity on her.

'Julie spent a few days in Scotland with Jonas just last week,' she said, and Nicholas's mouth dropped open in astonishment. 'The magazine she works for – *Peridot* – wanted an interview with the best-selling author of the month.'

'Good lord!' Nicholas stared across at Julie. 'I thought for a minute you were about to say Jonas and Julie were getting together again!'

'*Nicholas!*' Joanne nudged him impatiently, and he turned a little pink as his wife said: 'You stayed at the castle, Julie? How exciting! We've never even seen it, have we, Nick?'

'Well, I have. But it was years ago,' admitted Nicholas.

He gathered his composure. 'So you stayed with my illustrious brother, did you? What do you think of his blossoming writing career?'

'I – I think it's wonderful.' Julie concentrated on helping Penny to sip some orange juice from a beaker.

'Of course it is.' Joanne gave her husband another impatient look. 'And you've been doing awfully well, too, haven't you, Julie? I always read those things you do for *Peridot*. It's my favourite magazine.'

'Joanne buys them all,' remarked Nicholas laconically.

'I do not!' Joanne was indignant now, and even Julie had to smile at her sister-in-law's determined efforts to control her recalcitrant husband. They reminded her so much of the way she and Jonas used to behave and she wished with a desperation born of despair that she had not been so eager to continue with her career after their marriage. She could have worked on a part-time basis and thus avoided that overnight assignment which had resulted in such heartache. Jonas had never tried to stop her from working, he had always been adamant that marriage to him should not destroy any ambitions she might have. He had never suggested that they might start a family, but he had taken no precautions to prevent such a thing happening and it had been up to her to ensure that she never became pregnant. Only now, holding Joanne's baby in her arms, did she begin to appreciate exactly what she had denied herself.

After her son and his family had left, Mrs. Hunter telephoned Jonas's London apartment again. And again there was no reply.

Julie twisted her hands together when her mother-in-law put down the receiver, shaking her head. 'Do – do you think something is wrong?' she asked tremulously. 'It – it's after nine o'clock. Where could he possibly be? He's been out all day!'

Mrs. Hunter sighed. 'My dear child, he could be any number of places. And as he's alone, what has he got to rush home for? He could have gone out for lunch, and stayed for dinner.'

'But where? His agent's? A friend's?'

'He could be with his agent. I know he does visit with his family. He's godfather to their twin sons. Then there's Max Turnstall, that colleague of his from the *Chronicle*. He often goes there. Julie, you have to accept, after what happened yesterday, Jonas will avoid his own company!'

'I – I think I ought to go back—'

'Where? To London?' Mrs. Hunter sounded horrified.

'Yes. He – he may want to see me. If – if I'm there—'

'Julie, I know you. If you go back to London you'll hide from him. But you can't go on hiding all your life.'

Julie turned away, biting her lips. 'Mrs. Hunter, I – I know you know Jonas better than I do—'

'I wouldn't say that.'

'—but – but I just have this feeling that he – he won't ever want to see me again. I – I've tried to fool myself that it's not so. That he will forgive me. But I can't.' She lifted her shoulders and let them fall again. 'Can't you see? Today has proved it.'

'Why? Because he's out? Do you think he's with some woman, is that it?'

'No!' Julie turned. 'No, of course I don't think that. But – well, he has his life to lead, and I have mine. It's no use pretending we can forget the past . . .'

Mrs. Hunter caught her by the shoulders. 'Now you listen to me, young lady. You're going to go upstairs and get into bed, and I'll bring you another of my special nightcaps. It's late, and you're becoming morbid. In the morning everything will be different, you'll see!'

'I – I don't know—'

'Well, I do.' Mrs. Hunter pursed her lips. 'Now go along. And stop feeling sorry for yourself!'

Julie went obediently up the stairs, too depressed to offer any resistance. She washed, cleaned her teeth with her finger, and went into the bedroom. The nightgown she had worn the night before was lying on the bed and with unsteady fingers she unbuttoned her suit and blouse and took them off. Then she shed her underwear and pulled the cotton nightgown over her head.

She was brushing her hair before the dressing-table mirror when she heard the car turn into the drive and drone powerfully up to the door. Her heart catching in her throat she turned out the lights and went to the window. She peered down into the darkness. The car's headlamps were extinguished, but she would recognize the individual lines of the Porsche anywhere.

She pressed her fingers to her lips as the door swung open and Jonas got out, tall and disturbingly familiar in the light cast from the lounge windows. He slammed his door, mounted the steps and disappeared from sight.

She stood uncertainly, curling and uncurling her bare toes, and then tensing as the door downstairs opened and closed and she heard her mother-in-law's surprised greeting. But Jonas's reply was less than enthusiastic as he said abruptly, 'Julie's disappeared!'

'Julie's disappeared?' Mrs. Hunter spoke slowly, and Jonas went on: 'Yes – disappeared, vanished! I've been searching for her all day. God knows where she's gone! She not here, is she?'

Julie held her breath for a moment, and then Mrs. Hunter said: 'Here? Why should you think that?'

'Because I've tried everywhere else,' he muttered in a weary monotone. 'I didn't know where else to look, and I couldn't go back to the apartment, I couldn't!'

Julie heard the tortured note in his voice and responded to it instinctively, taking a few steps towards the door only to halt as Mrs. Hunter said: 'Have you seen her since I phoned you? Did you go to the flat?'

'Yes, yes. I went to the flat.' Julie moved to rest her cheek against the door jamb. 'But Angela was there. I had it out with her. God, I think I could have killed her. She was so sure of herself – of Julie! She practically admitted to sending the letter. But then everything went wrong – horribly wrong!'

'What do you mean?'

Julie heard Jonas expel his breath on a heavy sigh. 'Oh, well, Julie came back while we were arguing and Angela managed to convince her that I had come to try and force her to lie about our relationship. Haven't you noticed this?' Julie guessed he was indicating the scratch on his cheek. 'Angela did it.'

'But why? What did you do?'

'Me? Nothing!' Jonas sounded utterly defeated. 'You know Angela. She just wanted to show Julie how she had had to fight me off. Oh, it was all lies, lies! Julie just stood there like a bloody ghost! I can't tell you how I felt. I wanted to drag her out of there, by force if necessary. But I couldn't. When I touched her, she didn't want to know.'

'Are you sure?' Mrs. Hunter sounded concerned. 'She was probably shocked to find you there.'

'Yes, probably. Particularly the way Angela made it sound.'

'So what did you do?'

'What did I do?' Julie heard him utter an oath. 'I

walked out. I just walked out and left them to it.'

'I see.'

'I know I was wrong, you don't have to look at me like that. I know I should have stayed and tried to convince Julie that I'm not the swine she thinks me, but I felt so sick!' He sighed again. 'And now she's disappeared and I've been nearly out of my mind!'

'You – you say you've been looking for her? Why?'

'Why? *Why?* You know why. For God's sake, I love her, I need her! And no bloody female is going to keep us apart. One way or another I've got to show Julie I mean what I say.' He gave a short mirthless laugh. 'Who knows, I may have made her pregnant. She may need me after all.'

'But she's missing,' pointed out Mrs. Hunter quietly.

'Yes. Yes, I know.' Jonas's voice had thickened with his emotion. 'Angela doesn't know where she is. She's as concerned as I am, I think. And as for her mother . . . Well, she blames me, naturally And I can't altogether blame her for that.'

'Oh, Jonas!' Julie heard Mrs. Hunter's voice, eloquent with sympathy, and realized that she was not going to tell her son that Julie was there. It was up to Julie to do that.

On trembling legs she stepped out on to the landing and came to the top of the stairs. 'I'm here, Jonas,' she said clearly.

Jonas's head jerked upward and she felt a surge of compassion when she saw the red-rimmed eyes, the haggard expression he was wearing. He had shed his sheepskin jacket and the black shirt and pants he was wearing accentuated the unnatural pallor of his face.

'Julie!' he spoke disbelievingly, glancing almost blankly at his mother. Then he shook his head and mounted the stairs two at a time to reach her, dragging her roughly into his arms, burying his face in the heavy softness of her hair. 'Oh, *Julie!*' he groaned unsteadily. 'Thank God, you're here!'

Over his shoulder, Julie saw Mrs. Hunter disappear tactfully into the lounge, and when the door closed behind her Jonas swung Julie up into his arms and carried her into the bedroom which had been his since he was a very small boy . . .

Much later, Julie supposed it must be nearing midnight, Jonas swung his legs to the floor and sat on the side of the bed, stretching luxuriously. 'I'm hungry,' he stated, switching on the bedside lamp. 'Are you going to feed your prodigal husband?'

Julie sat up, too, smiling at him as she ran possessive hands over his shoulder, rested her chin on her fingers. 'I suppose I could,' she agreed lazily. 'Unless your mother is waiting to provide you with supper.'

'I somehow think that's not likely,' murmured Jonas, a little dryly. 'I'm sure she realizes that my wife is capable of providing everything I need.'

Julie's cheeks turned a little pink, and she slid off the bed and reached for the dressing gown which Mrs. Hunter had lent her. 'Yes, well – what do you want?'

'Julie?' Jonas caught her wrist, looking up at her strangely. 'You are coming back to me, aren't you? I mean, this wasn't just another experiment, was it?'

Julie shook her head, her lips pressed together to prevent them from trembling.

Jonas frowned. 'Then what is it? What's troubling you? Something is – I know it. Is it something my mother said?'

Julie shook her head again and then, with a little shudder, she said: 'Jonas, I have to tell you – Angela – Angela told me she'd been lying all along. I should hate you to hear that from someone else.'

'I know already.'

'You – know?' Julie felt hopelessly confused. 'But I don't understand.'

'Angela told me herself.'

'Angela?'

'Yes. This morning.' Jonas raised her fingers to his lips, kissing each of them in turn. 'I think she realized she had nothing to lose any more. She told me everything. She's terribly worried about you. I think she was half afraid you'd done something desperate.'

'So – so you know—?'

'That you intended coming back to me anyway? Yes. Yes, I know.' He looked up into her eyes. 'But you should have known all along that I would never do anything to hurt *you*!'

'Oh, Jonas!' Julie wanted to cry. It didn't seem possible after everything that had happened, after all the mistakes she had made, that she was being given a second chance. 'I love you!'

Jonas drew her against him, pressing his lips to the hollow between the opening lapels of her gown. 'Now,' he said, determinedly pushing her away from him, 'go and get me some food, woman! I'm starving! And as I have no intention of getting up for an early breakfast, you'd better get something for yourself as well . . .'

Romance
is
Beautiful

Get to the
HEART OF
HARLEQUIN

HARLEQUIN READER SERVICE is your passport to The Heart of Harlequin . . .

if You...

 enjoy the mystery and adventure of romance then you should know that Harlequin is the World's leading publisher of Romantic Fiction novels.

 want to keep up to date on all of our new releases, eight brand new Romances and four Harlequin Presents, each month.

 are interested in valuable re-issues of best-selling back titles.

 are intrigued by exciting, money-saving jumbo volumes.

 would like to enjoy North America's unique monthly Magazine "Harlequin" — available **ONLY** through Harlequin Reader Service.

are excited by **anything new** under the Harlequin sun.

then...

YOU should be on the Harlequin Reader Service — **INFORMATION PLEASE** list — it costs you nothing to receive our news bulletins and intriguing brochures. Please turn page for news of an **EXCITING FREE OFFER.**

a Special Offer for You...

just by requesting information on Harlequin Reader Service with absolutely no obligation, we will send you a "limited edition" copy, with a new, exciting and distinctive cover design — **VIOLET WINSPEAR'S** first Harlequin Best-Seller

LUCIFER'S ANGEL

You will be fascinated with this explosive story of the fast-moving, hard-living world of Hollywood in the 50's. It's an unforgettable tale of an innocent young girl who meets and marries a dynamic but ruthless movie producer. It's a gripping novel combining excitement, intrigue, mystery and romance.

A complimentary copy is waiting for YOU — just fill out the coupon on the next page and send it to us to-day.